The Mirage Compass

Adventure into the Hidden Unknown

Isha J.

Copyright © 2025 Isha J.

For Bir: fearless six-year-old explorer—my greatest inspiration and joy.

Table of Contents

The Attic's Secret

The attic had always been off-limits. Mira's grandmother, Amma, had made it clear that no one was to set foot in the old space at the top of the house. But today, curiosity got the better of her. Mira held her breath as she and Leo crept up the narrow staircase, the wood creaking softly under their weight. "Are you sure about this?" Leo whispered, glancing nervously over his shoulder.

"Keep your voice down!" Mira hissed back, clutching the flashlight tighter. "Do you want Amma to catch us?"

The air grew cooler as they neared the attic door, a faint smell of old wood and mystery seeping through the cracks. "You know this place is probably just full of junk, right?" Leo muttered, though his eyes darted around as if expecting something to leap out of the shadows.

Mira ignored him, her heart pounding with a mix of fear and excitement. She had spent years imagining what could be hidden up here: forgotten treasures, strange gadgets, or maybe even a map to something incredible. Now, as she placed her hand on the cold metal doorknob, her imagination ran wild.

"Ready?" she whispered.

Leo nodded, though his grip on the flashlight betrayed his nerves. Mira turned the knob slowly, and the door creaked open, revealing the attic's dim, shadowy interior.

"See? Just dusty old stuff," Leo said, his voice wavering as he scanned the room.

"We'll see," Mira whispered, her eyes narrowing as she spotted a large wooden crate in the corner. "Let's start there." Dust particles danced in the beam of the flashlight as they stepped inside. The space was cluttered with towering stacks of boxes and furniture draped in sheets, but something about the air felt… alive.

Their house was a small, cozy cottage on the edge of *Kalanya*, a town whispered about in old legends. Kalanya was a place where the mist lingered just a little longer in the mornings, and the trees seemed to hum with secrets carried by the wind. Surrounded by wildflower meadows and perched on a hill overlooking a sparkling lake, the cottage felt like it belonged in a storybook. The attic, with its creaky floorboards and cobwebbed corners, felt like a different world compared to the sunny rooms below.

It all started with a missing screwdriver. Leo, Mira's thirteen-year-old best friend and a self-proclaimed inventor, had been helping her fix an old birdhouse when the screwdriver mysteriously disappeared. As soon as her grandmother left for her afternoon walk, Mira and Leo climbed the narrow staircase, armed with a flashlight.

Mira crouched beside the old attic door, holding her breath as Leo knelt next to the rusted lock, a handmade key pinched between his fingers.

"You're sure this will work?" she whispered.

Leo gave her a sideways glance. "You've only asked me that six times." He slid the small, jagged-edged key into the lock. It clicked once, then stuck. Mira's eyes widened. Leo twisted it gently, and with a sudden metallic snap, the mechanism turned.

"Ha!" he grinned. "Told you—my best duplicate yet."

Mira gave him a proud nudge. "I knew pestering you would pay off."

The lock dropped away, and the door creaked open as they pushed it together, revealing a world of shadows and forgotten memories.

Boxes were piled haphazardly, their labels faded with age. A steamer trunk sat in one corner, and a broken rocking chair leaned against the far wall. Cobwebs shimmered in the faint light coming through a small round window.

"This place looks like it belongs in a ghost story," Leo said, sweeping his flashlight across the room. "Are you sure we're allowed up here?"

"Not really," Mira replied, stepping forward. Her sneakers squeaked on the wooden floorboards, kicking up little clouds of dust. "But Amma's not here, and we're not leaving until we find that screwdriver."

Leo sighed but followed her in.

As they searched through the boxes, Mira couldn't shake the feeling that the attic was hiding something important. She opened a box labelled "Books" and found a stack of old, leather-bound volumes. Another box held mismatched silverware and faded photographs.

"Anything yet?" Leo asked, his voice muffled as he looked through an old toolbox.

"Nothing useful," Mira said, brushing cobwebs off a small wooden chest. The chest was locked, its brass clasp dull with age.

She moved on, drawn to a large wooden crate shoved against the back wall. Something about it felt different. The crate was wrapped in a heavy tarp, and when Mira pulled it back, she saw an unusual symbol etched into the wood. It was a hexagon surrounded by a spiral pattern that seemed to flow outward, as if in motion. At the centre of the hexagon was a small, five-petaled flower with veins etched so finely they resembled a network of rivers. Tiny arrows pointed inward from each edge of the hexagon, converging toward the flower, giving the symbol an almost magnetic pull. The etching seemed to hum faintly, as if alive with energy, making it hard to look away.

"Leo, come look at this," Mira said, her voice low.

Leo joined her, shining his flashlight on the symbol. "Weird. Do you think it's some kind of family symbol?"

"I don't know," Mira said, running her fingers over the design. It felt strangely warm; as if it had been sitting in sunlight instead of the cold attic.

"What's inside?" Leo asked.

"Only one way to find out," Mira said, grabbing a nearby crowbar. With some effort, she pried the crate open. Inside was a leather-bound journal resting on a bed of faded blue velvet. The journal looked ancient, its corners worn and its cover embossed with the same strange symbol from the crate.

Mira picked it up carefully. It felt heavier than it looked, and the pages were filled with neat handwriting and detailed sketches when she opened it. One of the first pages had a name written in bold, looping letters:

Zorath Blackthorn

"Who's Zorath Blackthorn?" Leo asked, leaning over her shoulder.

Mira froze, her fingers hovering over the page. Her pulse quickened. That name—it echoed with the weight of stories whispered to her at bedtime, the kind wrapped in myth and mystery. Everyone in Kalanya had heard of Zorath Blackthorn—the legendary explorer said to have vanished chasing secrets too powerful for the world to know.

She blinked as if seeing the name for the first time all over again. "I… I know that name," she murmured, her voice barely above a whisper. "Amma used to talk about him in her stories. But I thought he was just a myth…" Her eyes scanned the aged script again, stunned. "Why would his journal be hidden in our attic?" Mira said, flipping through the journal. The pages were filled with maps, riddles, and strange symbols. One page had a drawing of what looked like a compass, but its face was marked with strange lines instead of numbers. Another page described something called the "Mirage Compass," said to reveal things hidden by time itself.

"Treasure?" Leo asked, his voice laced with playful curiosity.

"Who knows, but this is amazing," Mira whispered. "Why would Amma hide something like this?"

"Maybe she didn't want anyone to find it," Leo said, glancing nervously at the door.

Before Mira could respond, they heard the unmistakable sound of the front door creaking open. Amma was back.

"Quick, put it back!" Leo hissed.

But Mira couldn't stop looking at the journal. She'd only read a few pages, but it was enough to spark a curiosity she couldn't ignore. Reluctantly, she slipped the journal into her backpack, closed the crate, and covered it with the tarp again.

They hurried downstairs, brushing dust off their clothes just as Amma walked into the kitchen. She paused, her sharp gaze flicking between them.

"You two look like you've seen a ghost," she said, setting down her basket of vegetables. "Did you find the screwdriver?"

"Uh, no," Mira said quickly. "But we'll keep looking."

Amma raised an eyebrow but said nothing. As soon as she turned away, Mira and Leo exchanged a look.

"What are you going to do with the journal?" Leo whispered.

"I'm going to read it," Mira said firmly. "I think this is the start of something big."

And she was right. That night, as she sat on her bed with the journal open in her lap, Mira felt a thrill of excitement.

The attic had been hiding more than memories. It had been hiding a mystery—one that Mira was determined to uncover.

The Hidden Key

The next day, Mira wasted no time returning to the attic. She had spent the night studying Zorath Blackthorn's journal, but many pages were too cryptic to understand. One thing was clear—this wasn't just an ordinary book. It was a puzzle waiting to be solved.

Leo, as hesitant as he was, joined her again. "You're obsessed," he muttered, following her up the stairs.

Mira ignored him, her focus on the wooden crate she had seen the day before. She ran her fingers over its surface, tracing the same strange symbol that appeared in the journal. Something about it felt important.

Leo shifted uncomfortably. "You're not suggesting there's something important in there, are you? What if it's just old clothes?"

Mira ignored him, her gaze fixed on the wooden box inside. Unlike the other dusty, forgotten objects around it, this one felt *placed*. Deliberate. Almost as if it had been waiting for her to find it.

"What is it?" Leo asked, leaning closer.

"I don't know," Mira admitted. The box was about the size of a thick book, its surface worn smooth from years of handling. The same strange symbol from the crate was engraved on its lid, but this time, it was surrounded by a faint pattern of overlapping circles that looked almost like waves.

Mira lifted the box carefully, noting how light it felt. There was a small latch on the front, but it didn't budge when she tried to open it.

"Locked," she muttered, frustrated.

"Maybe that's a sign we should stop," Leo suggested, his voice rising slightly. "This is feeling... weird."

But Mira's curiosity had taken over completely. "Help me look for a key," she said, setting the box down gently and turning her attention to the clutter around them.

They sifted through the attic's contents, their movements stirring up dust clouds. Mira found a stack of yellowed letters tied with a red ribbon, an old globe with peeling maps, and a brass telescope. But no key.

Leo, meanwhile, unearthed a strange scroll box with frayed edges and faded gold lettering on the top. "Hey, check this out," he called.

Mira turned, brushing dust off her hands as she joined him. The title read *The Chronicles of Kalanya*.

"It's about the town," Leo said, flipping and checking the other side. "But this stuff looks ancient."

"Let me see," Mira said, leaning over his shoulder. It contained a hand-drawn map. The bottom left corner of the map caught her eye: it showed a drawing of the same symbol from the crate and the box, along with a passage written below it.

Mira squinted at the text. "It says, 'The flower at the centre marks the beginning, and the spiral leads the way. Only the worthy may find the path.'" She frowned. "What does that mean?"

Leo looked uneasy. "I don't like this. It's like some riddle."

"Exactly," Mira said, her excitement growing. "This is bigger than I thought. It's connected to our town. Possibly a map of ancient Kalanya."

Before Leo could protest, there was a faint clinking sound. Mira turned to see the small wooden box on the crate. The latch, which was firmly shut moments ago, now hung open.

"What did you do?" Leo asked, stepping back instinctively.

"Nothing," Mira whispered, her heart racing. She reached out cautiously and lifted the lid.

Inside, nestled in the silk lining, was a single object.

A *fragment* of something larger. It was a broken piece of metal and its shape looked like it was part of a circle, its edges rough where it had broken off from the rest. The surface was covered in fine, intricate etchings—symbols she didn't recognize, but ones that sent a thrill through her veins. It was a deep, shimmering blue, with faint veins of gold running through it like tiny rivers. It *glowed*, faintly, as if responding to her presence.

A strange sensation washed over Mira the moment her fingers closed around it. It was as if the attic itself had shifted. The air grew heavier, and the shadows seemed to deepen.

"Mira," Leo said, his voice trembling. "What's happening?"

"I... I don't know," Mira admitted. She held the metal piece up to the light, and for a split second, she thought she saw images flickering within it—scenes of lush forests, towering mountains, and a vast, glittering lake.

Then, just as suddenly as it had started, the sensation vanished. The attic was still again, and the metal piece in Mira's hand felt cool and inert.

Leo stared at her, his face pale. "We shouldn't have opened that."

Mira turned it over in her hand, her mind racing. "This isn't just any old attic junk," she said. "This is something important. Amma's been hiding it for a reason."

Leo sighed, running a hand through his hair. "And now we're in the middle of it."

Mira turned the metal over in her hands, feeling the cool weight of it. The engravings reminded her of something she had seen before.

Then it clicked.

She scrambled for Zorath's leather-bound journal, flipping through the pages until she found the sketch she was looking for.

It was a drawing of a compass—*the Mirage Compass*. But the face of the compass wasn't marked with numbers like a normal one. Instead, it had symbols. And at the edges of the sketch, there were empty spaces—*gaps*—exactly the shape of the piece she now held in her hand.

Her pulse quickened. "Leo… this is part of the Mirage Compass."

Leo blinked. "Wait, *what?*"

Mira stared down at the fragment, the realization sinking in. "This is why Amma kept the attic locked. She was hiding *this.*"

Leo hesitated. "Okay. Let's say that's true. What does it mean? What does this *compass* do?"

Mira shook her head. "I don't know yet. But if it was important enough to hide, then it has to be something *big.*"

Leo ran a hand through his hair. "Mira, did your grandmother *never* tell you about this? Not even once?"

"No," Mira admitted, a sinking feeling settling in her stomach. "But now I need to know *why*."

Before Leo could respond, they heard Amma calling out for them.

Leo's eyes widened. "We're so dead."

Mira stuffed the compass piece into her pocket, quickly covering the crate. The journal—she already had that tucked into her bag. But the scroll box—she couldn't leave it behind. On instinct, she grabbed it and slipped it into her bag.

Mira grabbed Leo's wrist, pulling him toward the attic door. "Come on!"

They scrambled down the steps as quietly as possible, barely reaching the hallway when Amma's voice rang out from the kitchen.

"Mira?"

Mira took a deep breath, forcing herself to sound normal. "Yeah, Amma?"

There was a pause. Then: "Did you find what you were looking for?"

Mira froze. Her heart thudded against her ribs. She quickly stepped away from the attic hatch, lowering her voice to sound like she was just a floor below.

"Yeah, we're in my room," she called, doing her best to keep it light. "Just… trying to build a few handy camping gadgets." The words tumbled out too fast, a little too rehearsed, but she forced a small laugh at the end to make it sound natural.

Leo raised an eyebrow but stayed silent, listening.

Amma didn't reply right away. Then, softly, "Lunch will be ready soon. Just don't leave your things lying around."

Mira let out a shaky breath, her fingers tightening around the compass piece. "Okay."

Leo leaned in and whispered, "That was *way* too close."

Mira nodded, but her thoughts were elsewhere.

She had *Zorath Blackthorn's* journal. And now, she had a compass piece and an ancient map.

Something told her that whatever she had just uncovered… was only the beginning.

The First Clue

Mira rotated on her foot; eyes locked on Leo as he lunged forward. She ducked at the last second, feeling the air shift as his punch whistled past her ear.

"Too slow," she taunted, flipping backward to regain her stance.

Leo groaned, rolling his shoulders. "Yeah, yeah. Maybe if you spent less time reading ancient journals and more time teaching me how to dodge like that, I'd actually stand a chance."

Mira smirked. "Maybe you should spend less time inventing weird gadgets and more time practicing."

Their instructor's voice cut through the air. "Mira, Leo, focus!"

Both snapped their attention forward, adjusting their stances. Their Kung Fu class took place in a small dojo near the town centre, where soft mats covered the floor, and the scent of polished wood and sweat hung in the air. The other students were practicing drills along the perimeter, but Mira and Leo had been paired together for sparring.

As they circled each other, Mira's mind wasn't just on the fight. It was on the puzzle they had uncovered the night before—the *Mirage Compass*, Zorath Blackthorn's *journal*, the *mysterious map*. She had barely gotten any sleep, replaying Amma's bedtime stories in her head, searching for hidden clues.

Leo must have been thinking the same thing because when he ducked left, only to step back, he muttered, "So, what's your guess on 'the flower at the centre marks the beginning'?"

Mira caught his movement and countered effortlessly, knocking his wrist aside. "No idea yet. But it has to be a symbol. Maybe something in town?"

Leo launched a high kick, which Mira ducked with ease. "And what about 'only the worthy may find the path'?"

Mira hesitated for just a second—just enough for Leo to sweep her legs from under her. She hit the mat with a *thud*, coughing as the air rushed out of her lungs.

Leo grinned down at her. "Distraction. Works every time."

Mira groaned, rubbing her elbow. "Okay, okay, I deserved that one."

Their instructor clapped his hands. "Good work, you two. Switch partners!"

As they bowed to each other and moved aside, Leo whispered, "We need to figure this out. Tonight."

Mira nodded. She had the same thought.

A Breakfast of Memories

The scent of cardamom and sizzling butter greeted them as they walked into the house. The morning sun spilled golden light through the kitchen windows, casting a warm glow over the wooden table, where Amma was setting down a fresh plate of *appam* and *kadala curry*, the coconut-laced aroma filling the air.

Leo inhaled deeply, flopping into a chair. "Your grandmother's cooking is *legendary*."

Amma chuckled, setting a cup of *sulaimani* tea in front of Mira. "And yet, every time you visit, you eat like you've never been fed before."

Mira grinned as she reached for a piece of *appam*, tearing it with her fingers. Leo had been coming to spend summers at their home since they were six years old. His mother had been her mother's best friend, and after Mira's parents had passed away, Amma had insisted he always had a place here.

"Didn't get food like this back home," Leo said through a mouthful. "Mom's an *okay* cook, but nothing compared to you, Amma."

Mira laughed, but as she sipped her tea, her mind wandered to the journal. To the compass piece now tucked safely in her room. To the fact that Amma had hidden it all this time.

She hesitated, then asked, "Amma… do you ever think about them?"

Amma's hands, busy pouring another cup of tea, slowed slightly. But she didn't falter. "Every day," she said softly. "Your parents were the brightest lights in my life."

Leo glanced at Mira. "I wish I had known them better."

"They would've liked you," Amma said with a small smile. "Especially your knack for getting into trouble."

Leo beamed. "That's a family trait, I think."

Mira played with the rim of her cup. "Did they ever… talk about Kalanya's history? About the old legends?"

Amma raised an eyebrow. "I see where this is going."

Leo leaned forward. "Come on, Amma. You always told Mira those crazy bedtime stories about lost cities and secret treasures. Any chance there was truth to them?"

Amma smiled knowingly. "Stories always have a bit of truth, but the real question is—what are you really asking?"

Mira hesitated, then shook her head. "Just curious."

"Curiosity," Amma mused. "That's the same thing that got Zorath Blackthorn in trouble."

Mira's pulse quickened, but Amma simply continued sipping her tea.

Leo shot her a look. They both knew that wasn't just a passing remark.

Something about Amma's stories, about the attic's secrets, was connected.

And they *had* to find out what.

Piecing the Clues Together

Later that evening, Mira and Leo sat cross-legged on the floor of her room, surrounded by scattered papers, books, and the dim glow of the desk lamp. The map lay open in Mira's lap, the inscription staring back at them:

"The flower at the centre marks the beginning, and the spiral leads the way. Only the worthy may find the path."

The compass piece gleamed faintly beside her, and the journal rested against her knee.

Leo groaned, running a hand through his messy hair. "We've been at this for hours, and I still don't get it."

Mira sighed, flipping through Zorath's journal again, her fingers brushing over the worn pages. Suddenly, she froze.

"Wait—Leo, look!" She jabbed her finger at a passage written in Zorath's neat, slanted handwriting. "This isn't just the same phrase—it's slightly different!"

Leo leaned in. "What do you mean?"

Mira read aloud: *"The flower at the centre… find the path where the roots touch the past."*

She sat back, her pulse quickening. "This changes everything. What if 'flower' isn't a literal flower?"

Leo muttered. "Then what else could it be?"

Mira grabbed the map of old Kalanya, her heart pounding as she traced her finger along its faded surface. She scanned the forests, the rivers, the trails—until her eyes locked on a familiar shape.

"This," she whispered, pointing. "This is the centre of the forest."

Leo squinted at the parchment, then his eyes widened. "No way."

His finger stabbed at the marking near the heart of the forest.

"The old oak tree," he breathed.

Mira's skin prickled with excitement. "It's not just any oak tree—it's been there for centuries, untouched by time."

Leo sat back, exhaling sharply. "The flower at the centre marks the beginning..." he repeated. "The oak tree *is* the flower. It's the starting point."

Mira felt a rush of energy. "Then that's where we need to go next."

Leo grinned. "And the spiral?"

Mira's fingers brushed the map again, her eyes narrowing. There—subtle but visible—a spiral pattern in the way the forest trails wound around the oak tree.

"The forest itself," she whispered. "It was built *around* the tree. That's what the inscription meant."

Leo let out a low whistle. "Okay. That's… kinda genius."

Mira's mind raced. Amma had told her bedtime stories about a lost path in the forest. Stories of a hidden secret buried beneath an ancient tree. Could it have been a clue all along?

Leo clapped his hands together. "Alright. Tomorrow, we go to the forest. And whatever that waits beneath that ancient tree…"

Mira nodded, but a strange unease settled in her chest.

Something told her this was no ordinary clue.

The Call of the Mountain

The first rays of dawn filtered through the thin curtains in Mira's room, painting the walls in soft hues of pink and gold. She sat by her window, the journal open in her lap, her thoughts racing. Leo, still half-asleep, was sprawled on the rug, a blanket draped over him. The events of the previous night replayed in her mind: the attic, the journal, the glowing map. It was all so surreal, yet undeniably real.

"Leo," Mira whispered, nudging him gently with her foot. "Wake up. We need to get ready."

Leo groaned and rolled onto his side, his hair sticking out in every direction. "It's barely morning. Can't this wait?"

"No," Mira said firmly. "If Amma catches us, we're done. We have to leave before she wakes up."

That got Leo's attention. He sat up, rubbing his eyes. "Alright, alright. But I still think this is a bad idea."

"Noted," Mira said with a grin. She closed the journal and slid it into her backpack, along with a flashlight, a water bottle, and a few snacks. "Let's go."

The house was silent as they crept downstairs, their footsteps muffled on the old wooden floors. Amma's door was closed, and Mira could hear the faint sound of her breathing. She paused for a moment, guilt tugging at her, but the pull of the journal was stronger.

Moving quickly, she grabbed a notepad from the kitchen counter and scribbled a message:

"Gone camping for a few days. Be back soon. Love you, Amma!"

She tore off the page and stuck it under the fridge magnet shaped like a tiny compass—one of Amma's favourite keepsakes. Taking a deep breath, she stepped back, hoping it would be enough to ease any worry. Then, without another glance, she turned and followed Leo out.

Outside, the air was crisp and cool, carrying the earthy scent of dew-soaked grass. Kalanya stretched before them, its winding cobblestone streets quiet in the early morning light. Beyond the town, the forest loomed, its dense canopy shrouded in mist. And beyond that, the ridge—their destination—rose against the sky, bathed in the soft glow of sunrise.

"Are you sure about this?" Leo asked as they started down the hill.

Mira nodded. "If Amma didn't want us to know about the journal, it's because it's important. I need to know why."

The path to the forest was overgrown but familiar. They'd spent countless summers exploring the outskirts, searching for hidden streams and climbing trees. But today, the forest felt different. The shadows seemed deeper; the air heavier.

"This place gives me the creeps," Leo muttered, sticking close to Mira.

"Don't be a baby," she teased, though she couldn't shake the feeling that they were being watched.

They followed the map's guidance, using the landmarks drawn in the journal to navigate. The spiral had pointed them to a small clearing with an ancient oak tree at its centre. Its gnarled branches stretched out like skeletal arms, and the ground beneath it was littered with fallen leaves.

"This is it," Mira said, flipping through journal pages and comparing the drawings and descriptions to their surroundings. "The path to the mountain starts here."

"I don't see a path," Leo said, looking around. "Just a lot of trees."

Mira knelt by the base of the oak, brushing away leaves and dirt. Her fingers found a smooth stone embedded in the ground, its surface engraved with the same symbol from the journal.

"Look," she said, pointing it out to Leo. "This has to be it."

As she touched the stone, a low hum filled the air. Leo stumbled back, his eyes wide. "What did you do?"

Before Mira stood up in shock. The leaves rustled as if caught in an unseen breeze, and the stone began to glow faintly. A thin line of light appeared, snaking away from the oak tree and disappearing into the forest.

"It's a trail," Mira whispered, her heart racing. "Come on."

"Wait, wait," Leo said, grabbing her arm. "We don't know where this leads. What if it's dangerous?"

"We'll never know if we don't follow it," Mira said, her voice steady. "You can stay here if you want, but I'm going."

Leo hesitated, then sighed. "Fine. But if we die, I'm blaming you."

The light led them deeper into the forest, winding between towering trees and over moss-covered rocks. The further they went, the quieter it became. Even the birds seemed to hold their breath.

After what felt like hours, they emerged into another clearing. At its centre stood a stone archway, weathered and overgrown with ivy. The symbol from the journal was etched into the keystone, its edges glowing faintly.

"This is it," Leo said, stepping closer. "This is where the map leads."

Mira frowned. "It's just an old arch. What are we supposed to do with it?"

She studied the journal again, her fingers tracing the words beneath the map: "The key to the past lies within the heart of Kalanya. Follow the path, but tread lightly, for some doors are meant to stay closed."

"I think we're supposed to go through it," she said, her voice barely above a whisper.

"Through it?" Leo repeated. "It's not even a door."

"Not a physical one," Mira said, stepping closer to the arch. She hesitated for a moment, then reached out to touch the symbol. The instant her fingers made contact, the air around them shimmered, and the archway filled with a swirling light.

Leo stumbled back. "What… what is that?"

Mira's heart pounded in her chest. "I don't know. But I think it's where we're supposed to go."

"You're insane," Leo said, but he didn't stop her as she stepped forward, the light reflecting in her wide eyes.

She held up the map, scanning it carefully—but then she froze. The lines and markings that had guided them this far simply… stopped. No more routes, no more landmarks. Just a blank space where the path should have continued.

Leo sulked. "Wait… that's it? The map just *ends*?"

Mira tilted her head, amusement flickering across her face. "I guess that means we're officially off the map." "Guess that means we get to make our own path," she said, rolling up the map. "That sounds like the best part of the adventure to me."

Taking a deep breath, Mira turned to Leo and held out her hand. "Come with me."

Leo hesitated, fear and curiosity warring on his face. Finally, he took her hand. "If we die, I'm haunting you."

Mira laughed softly. "Deal."

Together, they stepped into the light. For a moment, there was nothing but a blinding brilliance, a sensation of weightlessness. Then, the world shifted, and they were somewhere else entirely.

The forest was gone. They stood on the edge of a vast, shimmering lake, its waters reflecting a sky filled with two suns. Towering mountains loomed in the distance, their peaks glowing with an otherworldly light. The air was warm and fragrant, filled with the sound of gentle waves lapping at the shore.

Leo stared in awe. "Where are we?"

Mira didn't answer. She was too busy staring at the mountain in the distance, the one mentioned in the journal. Somehow, she knew this was only the beginning.

The Next Clue

The shimmering lake stretched endlessly before them, its surface glowing gold and silver under the light of the twin suns. Mira stepped closer to the edge, the sand soft beneath her boots. The towering mountain in the distance stood like a beacon, and though she couldn't explain it, she knew they were meant to be here.

"This place is amazing," Leo said, his voice low with wonder. He crouched to touch the water, pulling his hand back quickly when the surface glowed faintly. "Okay, that's... weird."

Mira pulled the journal from her bag, flipping to the sketch of the lighthouse. Underneath the drawing were the words: *The first step reveals the path. Trust the compass.*

"Look at this," she said, holding the journal open to show Leo. "It's a lighthouse. We have to find it."

"A lighthouse in the middle of a lake? Sure, why not," Leo muttered, but his curiosity was visibly high.

Mira scanned the shoreline, her eyes catching a faint trail of stones leading into the lake. Each stone was carved with patterns that seemed to glow faintly; as if responding to the sun's light.

"There." Mira pointed. "A path."

Leo looked in amazement. "A path into the water? That doesn't exactly scream 'safe.'"

"It's our only clue," Mira replied. She stepped onto the first stone, her heart pounding. The stone was cool and firm beneath her feet, and the water rippled gently around it. She turned to Leo, who was still standing on the shore.

"Are you coming?" she asked.

Leo hesitated, then sighed. "Have to do this!"

Together, they followed the path. Each step revealed more glowing patterns on the stones, and the air grew warmer, filled with a faint hum that seemed to come from the lake itself. Mira felt a mix of excitement and fear, her grip tightening on the journal as they neared the end of the path.

The lighthouse emerged from the water like a ghost from the past. Its weathered walls were covered in moss and carvings, and it leaned slightly to one side as if it had been standing there for centuries. A narrow dock connected the path to the lighthouse, the wood creaking under their weight as they stepped onto it.

"This is it," Mira whispered, her eyes wide as they reached the door. It was slightly open, and she pushed it open, revealing a dim, dusty interior.

The air inside was thick and salty, and the walls were lined with shelves holding old books, rusted tools, and jars filled with strange, murky liquids. A spiral staircase wound upward, its steps uneven and worn. At the centre of the room stood a pedestal, much like the one in the cave, and an ornate box rested on it.

"That has to be the clue," Mira said, stepping toward the pedestal. The box was carved with the same patterns as the stones outside, and it seemed to hum faintly, as if alive.

"Wait," Leo said, grabbing her arm. "What if it's a trap?"

"We don't have a choice," Mira said, shaking him off. She reached out and lifted the lid of the box. Inside was another compass piece, identical to the one they'd found before but engraved with different symbols. Beside it lay a scrap of parchment, its edges worn with age.

Mira unfolded the parchment carefully, her eyes scanning the handwritten words:

The desert sun reveals the truth. Seek the mirage that guides the way.

"A desert?" Leo said, peering over her shoulder. "Great. Because nothing says 'fun' like a trek through a deadly wasteland."

Before Mira could respond, the ground beneath them began to shake. The jars rattled on their shelves, and the hum in the air grew louder, turning into a deafening roar. Mira grabbed the compass piece and parchment, shoving them into her bag.

"We need to get out of here!" Leo shouted, pulling Mira toward the door.

They stumbled out onto the dock as the water around the lighthouse began to churn violently. Dark shapes moved beneath the surface, their forms massive and menacing.

"Run!" Leo yelled, and they sprinted back along the stone path. The waves crashed against the stones, and the air filled with the sound of splintering wood as the dock collapsed behind them.

By the time they reached the shore, the path had vanished beneath the water. Mira turned back, watching in awe and fear as the lighthouse sank slowly into the lake, its light flickering once before disappearing completely.

"What just happened?" Leo panted, his hands on his knees.

"I don't know," Mira admitted, her chest heaving. She clutched her bag tightly, the compass piece pressing against her side. "But we have our next clue. The desert."

Leo groaned. "Of course, it's a desert. Why couldn't it be something simple, like a park or a library?"

Mira managed a small smile, despite the tension still thrumming through her. "Come on. We need to figure out where this desert is."

As they made their way to the mountain, the twin suns casting long shadows on the ground, Mira still couldn't shake the feeling that they were being watched. She glanced over her shoulder, but there was nothing there—only the shimmering lake and the faint outline of the sinking lighthouse.

"We'll figure this out," she said softly, more to herself than to Leo. "We have to."

Leo didn't reply, but his determined expression said he was with her. Together, they walked on, the parchment's riddle and the mystery of the compass driving them forward knowing that the challenges might get bigger.

The Reclusive Mapmaker

The parchment's riddle led them to a town nestled at the base of the mountain: Sandrift. The name made Leo grunt as they trudged through the dusty streets, already dreading the desert journey ahead. Sandrift was a mix of crumbling adobe homes and wooden shacks, and it had a sense of abandonment as if most of its residents had long since given up on it.

"I can't believe we're looking for a mapmaker," Leo said, scanning the empty streets. "Who even uses maps anymore?"

"People who don't want to get lost in a desert," Mira replied, holding the journal tightly. The parchment they'd found in the lighthouse had been clear: *The desert sun reveals the truth. Seek the mirage that guides the way.* But the mirage could be anywhere in the vast, deadly sands, and they needed help to find it.

After escaping the lighthouse, Mira found a faded note tucked inside the journal. Now, as they walked, she kept murmuring the words under her breath, almost like a mantra. *"Seek the cartographer in Sandrift; they know the paths others do not."*

Leo shot her a look. "You think repeating it a hundred times will make the answer appear?"

Mira exhaled sharply. "No… but I feel like if I stop saying it, I'll forget how important it is." She clutched the journal tighter. "Whoever this cartographer is, they might be the only one who can help us now." The words brought back a vivid memory of her grandmother's bedtime stories about hidden maps and the secretive people who made them.

"Why do they hide?" a younger Mira had asked.

Amma had smiled knowingly. "Because the greatest maps lead to treasures some would rather keep buried."

Now, those words echoed in her mind as she and Leo turned another corner. The note had been their only lead, and as the heat of the sun pressed down on them, Mira wondered if they were chasing shadows.

Leo wiped the sweat from his forehead. "How are we supposed to find someone who might not want to be found?"

Mira pulled the journal from her satchel, flipping to the page where the note had been tucked. "They'll find us," she said, more to convince herself than Leo. "If they're as secretive as Amma hinted in the bedtime stories, they're probably already watching."

"That's not creepy at all," Leo muttered.

They reached a quieter part of the town, where the streets narrowed and the bustling crowd thinned to a few scattered figures. Mira's eyes were drawn to a weathered wooden sign hanging above a door: a compass etched into its surface, but the needle pointed in impossible directions, spinning ever so slightly as if alive.

Leo noticed it too. "That's… strange."

"Here." Mira pointed to a small rusted plate below the sign. It read *Cartography and Curiosities* in faded letters. "This has to be it."

Leo raised an eyebrow. "Cartography *and* curiosities? Sounds like we're about to meet someone strange."

Mira approached the door and knocked. For a moment, nothing happened. Then, the door creaked open just enough for a pair of sharp eyes to peer out. A voice, dry and cautious, spoke. "What do you want?"

Mira hesitated, clutching the journal. "We were told to find the mapmaker. Someone who knows the paths others don't."

The door opened wider, revealing a young boy, no older than sixteen, with wild, untamed hair, ink-stained hands, and a wary expression. He wore glasses that slipped down his nose as he studied them with suspicion.

He looked at Mira, then at Leo, his gaze lingering on the journal in her hands. "Who told you about me?"

Mira faltered. "It's… complicated. But we need your help."

The boy—Kai, as they later learned—studied them for a long moment before stepping aside. "Come in."

The inside of the shop was dim and cramped, filled with shelves overflowing with scrolls, maps, and strange trinkets. The right wall was lined with maps of every size and style. Some were ancient, their edges curling and the ink faded; others were vibrant. A faint smell of ink and old parchment hung in the air. A large table dominated the centre of the room, cluttered with parchment, quills, and tools Mira couldn't name.

"You're not the first to come looking for me," Kai said, crossing his arms. "But most don't make it past the door."

Leo raised an eyebrow. "Should we be flattered?"

Kai ignored him, focusing on Mira. "What do you want?" he asked bluntly.

"Are you the mapmaker," Mira asked back.

The boy crossed his arms. "Depends on who's asking."

Leo rolled his eyes. "Great, a kid with a wary attitude. This should be fun."

Mira stepped forward, ignoring Leo. She pulled the parchment from her bag and unfolded it. "We found this. It says we need to find a mirage in the desert. We were told you might be able to help."

Kai glanced at the parchment, his eyes narrowing. Then, without a word, he snatched it from her hands and examined it closely. "This is old. Very old," he muttered, more to himself than to them. "Where did you get it?"

"Does it matter?" Mira said, keeping her tone even. "Can you help us or not?"

Kai looked up at her, his expression unreadable. "Why should I? People don't just wander into Sandrift looking for mirages unless they're trouble."

"We're not trouble," Mira insisted. "We're trying to solve a mystery. This compass"—she pulled the piece from her bag— "is part of it. We think it's connected to the desert. Please, we need your help."

Kai's eyes widened slightly at the sight of the compass piece, but he quickly masked his surprise. "The desert isn't a game," he said, his voice sharp. "People go in and don't come out. And if you're not careful, you'll end up just like them."

"We'll take that risk," Leo said, stepping forward. "But we can't do it without a guide. Someone who knows this desert better than anyone."

Kai hesitated, glancing between them and the compass piece. His expression darkened. "The desert is no place for travellers. Its mirages have driven even the most seasoned wanderers mad."

"We don't have a choice," Mira said. "Please. You're our only hope."

Kai looked at the compass piece again, and then at the journal cover page through Mira's fingers. Something flickered in his eyes—recognition, perhaps, or curiosity. Finally, he sighed. "If I help you, it's not because I think you'll make it. It's because I'm tired of hiding. But don't say I didn't warn you."

He disappeared into the back of the shop and returned moments later with a large, rolled-up map. He spread it out on a nearby table, revealing a detailed layout of the desert. Symbols and notes were scribbled in the margins, and certain areas were marked with red ink.

"This is the Mirage Expanse," Kai said, pointing to a vast section of the map. "It's full of shifting sands and optical illusions. Even with a map, it's easy to get lost."

"What about this?" Mira asked, pointing to a red circle on the map.

Kai's jaw tightened, and his gaze grew serious. "That's the centre of the expanse. The locals call it the Glassheart. They say it's where the sun burns the brightest and the mirages are the most dangerous. If your mirage is anywhere, it's there."

"Then that's where we're going," Mira said firmly.

Kai looked at her like she'd lost her mind. "You can't just walk into the Glassheart. You'll need supplies, water, and a way to navigate the sandstorms. And even then, it's a death trap."

"We'll figure it out," Mira said, her determination unwavering. "Do you have any advice?"

Kai hesitated, then nodded. "Trust your instincts. The mirages mess with your mind, but if you stay focused, you'll see what's real. And whatever you do, don't let fear take over. That's how people get lost."

Leo, ever the sceptic, leaned against the cluttered table and studied the young mapmaker with a raised eyebrow. "So, what's the deal with you? You're barely older than us, but you're supposed to be this legendary mapmaker? No offense, but you don't exactly scream 'expert.'"

Kai shot him a sharp glance, clearly annoyed. "Age doesn't determine skill," he replied curtly, rolling up the map he had just shown them. "And for the record, I've been doing this for longer than you'd think."

"Longer than we'd think?" Leo pressed, smirking. "What, did you start charting the world as a toddler?"

Mira gave Leo a warning look, but Kai sighed and crossed his ink-stained arms. "If you must know, my family has been cartographers for generations. My father was one of the best—he mapped parts of the Mirage Expanse no one had ever returned from. Everything I know, I learned from him."

Leo's smirk faded slightly, and Mira leaned forward, curious. "What happened to him?" she asked gently.

Kai hesitated, his gaze flicking to the map in his hands. For a moment, his confidence slipped, replaced by something more vulnerable. "He went too deep into the Glassheart," Kai said quietly. "Chasing a mirage, he thought held the key to the desert's secrets. He never came back."

The room fell silent. Even Leo seemed at a loss for words.

"I took over after that," Kai continued, his voice steady but tinged with sadness. "I was seven and have spent days and nights studying his notes, refining the maps he left behind, and learning everything I could about the desert. People think the Mirage Expanse is impossible to understand, but they're wrong. It's dangerous, yes, but if you know where to look, it can be navigated."

Mira nodded, a newfound respect for Kai taking root. "And you've never been to the Glassheart yourself?"

Kai shook his head. "No. My father always said it was a place of no return. But if you're determined to go there, I'll guide you. Not because I think it's a good idea, but because it might be the only way to uncover the truth."

Leo scratched the back of his head, looking sheepish. "Alright, I take it back. You're not just some kid. You've got guts."

Kai snorted. "And you're not just some loudmouth. You've got... well, not much, but maybe potential."

Leo grinned. "I'll take it."

Mira smiled, grateful for the brief moment of light-heartedness. "Thank you, Kai."

Kai met her gaze and nodded. "Just be ready. The desert doesn't forgive mistakes."

He paused, then added reluctantly, "I'll come with you. If you're serious about this, you'll need someone who knows what they're doing."

Mira blinked in surprise. "You'd do that?"

Kai shrugged. "Someone has to make sure you don't get yourselves killed. Besides, I've always wanted to see the Glassheart for myself."

Leo grinned. "Looks like we've got our mapmaker."

Kai rolled up the map and tucked it under his arm. "Meet me at the edge of town at sunrise. Bring everything you need, because once we're in the desert, there's no turning back."

As they left the shop, Mira couldn't help but feel a surge of hope. They had a guide, a map, and a destination. The desert would be dangerous, but she knew they were one step closer to uncovering the truth.

Still, as they walked through the quiet streets of Sandrift, she felt the lingering unease that they were being watched. She looked back, but the shadows remained still and silent.

"Everything okay?" Leo asked.

"Yeah," Mira said, forcing a smile. "Let's just get ready for tomorrow."

Deep down, though, she knew what lay ahead would test them in ways she couldn't imagine.

Desert of Deceptions

As the first light of dawn broke over Sandrift, Mira, Leo, and Kai stood at the edge of the vast desert. The Mirage Expanse stretched endlessly before them, a sea of golden dunes rippling under the morning sun. Despite the early hour, the air was already thick with heat.

Kai tightened the straps on his satchel, his face serious. "Last chance to turn back. Once we're in, there's no room for hesitation."

Mira met his gaze with unwavering determination. "We're ready."

Leo adjusted his hat, shading his eyes from the sun. "Ready as we'll ever be."

With that, they set off into the desert, the town of Sandrift disappearing behind them. The sand shifted beneath their feet, making every step a struggle. The only sounds were the crunch of their boots and the occasional gust of wind.

The Mirage Expanse lived up to its name—shifting dunes and shimmering heat played tricks on their eyes, distorting reality at every step. Kai led the way, his map clutched tightly in one hand, while Mira and Leo followed, their canteens rattling against their packs.

Hours passed, and the sun climbed higher, turning the desert into a furnace. Mira wiped the sweat from her brow. "How much further until we reach the observatory ruins?"

Kai glanced at the map he had spread over his arm. "If we keep this pace, we should see it by sunset. But the Mirage Expanse has a way of... distorting things. Stay focused."

As they trudged on, the desert began to play tricks on them. The horizon shimmered, bending and twisting in unnatural ways. At one point, Leo stopped abruptly, pointing at what appeared to be a lush oasis in the distance. "Water! Finally!"

Kai grabbed his arm. "It's a mirage. Don't waste your energy chasing illusions."

Leo frowned but nodded, his enthusiasm dampened. They pressed on, the heat and disorientation taking their toll.

By midday, the first hallucination struck. Mira gasped as she saw a figure in the distance that looked strikingly like her grandmother. The figure waved, beckoning her closer.

"Amma?" Mira whispered, stepping forward.

Kai's voice cut through the haze. "It's not real, Mira! Focus!"

She stopped, her heart pounding. The figure vanished, leaving nothing but empty sand. Shaken, she tightened her grip on the compass pieces.

"I swear I saw a caravan," Leo muttered, wiping sweat from his forehead. "How are we supposed to know what's real?"

"Trust your instincts," Kai replied without looking back. "The mirages mess with your mind. Focus on what doesn't change—the position of the sun, and the patterns in the sand. That's how you stay grounded."

Mira glanced at her compass piece, its metallic surface reflecting the sunlight. "And the mirages—are they always random?"

Kai hesitated. "Not always. Sometimes they're warnings."

Hours later, the trio finally spotted the observatory ruins as the sun dipped lower in the sky. Perched atop a pointed outcrop of rock, the crumbling structure looked ancient and weathered, its walls partially buried in sand. A sense of foreboding hung in the air. Its once-proud dome was cracked and weathered, and its walls seemed to sag under the weight of time. "This is it," Kai said, his voice low. "The next piece of the compass is supposed to be here."

They climbed the rocky incline, their legs aching from the effort. Their steps echoed in the spooky silence. Inside, the observatory was a maze of broken walls and collapsed ceilings. Faded carvings covered the remaining walls, their intricate designs hinting at long-lost knowledge.

In the centre of the main chamber stood a pedestal, its surface etched with a riddle:

In the land where the sun burns bright, a shadow reveals the guiding light.

Mira read the riddle aloud, tilting her head in confusion. "What does it mean?"

Kai examined the carvings around the room. "It's about shadows. We need to figure out how they're supposed to guide us."

As the last rays of sunlight filtered through a carefully carved opening in the ceiling, a beam of light hit the pedestal, casting a shadow on the floor. The shadow stretched to the entrance, and another faint shadow stretched from the doorway, pointing directly at a nearby wall. Mira paused, dumbfounded. "Is it just me, or does that shadow look... deliberate?"

Kai followed her gaze, his brow furrowing. "You're right. Shadows like that don't just happen." He knelt to study the markings near the doorway. "It's a clue. My father used to say the desert reveals its secrets in layers. We're meant to follow it."

They traced the shadow's path, which led them to a section of the wall partially buried in sand. Together, they cleared it, revealing faint carvings etched into the stone.

Leo pointed. "That's got to be it."

Symbols adorned the walls—intricate carvings that seemed to pulse faintly. Mira's eyes darted across the designs, her fingers itching to touch them, but she hesitated. "These symbols... they look familiar, but I can't place them." She instantly took out the journal and started tossing its pages.

Kai stepped closer, pulling a small leather notebook from his satchel. Its edges were frayed, and its pages were filled with his father's meticulous notes. He flipped through them, muttering to himself. "These markings... they're part of an old navigation system. My father mentioned something about them in his notes."

Leo leaned against the wall, panting. "Care to share with the class? Because right now, it looks like gibberish to me."

Kai shot him a glare but continued. "These symbols represent constellations. The observatory must have been used to map the stars, but they're more than just decorative. They're a puzzle."

Mira stepped forward, pointing to a series of interlocking circles. "This one—it matches the compass piece."

Kai nodded. "Exactly. It might reveal something if we align the symbols with the compass."

They worked together, Kai deciphering the notes while Mira and Leo adjusted the symbols on the wall. Sweat dripped down their faces as they strained to align the carvings. Finally, a faint click echoed through the chamber.

"Did we just... solve it?" Leo asked, his voice tinged with disbelief.

Mira pressed the circular symbol that matched the compass piece. For a moment, nothing happened. Then, the wall trembled, and a hidden compartment slid open, revealing a piece of the compass, its metallic surface gleaming in the dim light.

Mira carefully retrieved it, holding it up for the others to see. "We did it," she said, a smile breaking through her exhaustion.

Kai's expression was cautious. "We're not out of danger yet. The desert doesn't like giving up its secrets so easily."

As if on cue, a deep rumble echoed through the ruins. The ground beneath their feet began to tremble.

"What did you do?" Leo shouted; his voice panicked.

Mira looked around with her heart racing. "I don't know!"

A deep rumble shook the observatory, and cracks snaked across the floor and walls. Sand began to pour in through the fissures, and the entire structure groaned as if on the verge of collapse.

Kai grabbed the map and stuffed it into his bag. "We need to get out of here. Now!"

The trio sprinted toward the entrance as the ground cracked beneath their feet. A massive chunk of the ceiling collapsed behind them, sending a cloud of dust and debris into the air. Mira stumbled, but Leo caught her arm, pulling her forward.

They leaped over widening gaps in the floor, their lungs burning from the effort. At one point, a cascade of sand poured from above, nearly burying Kai. He clawed his way free, coughing but unrelenting.

The exit loomed ahead, but the path was treacherous. A sudden burst of wind howled through the observatory, stirring up sand and blinding them. Mira shielded her face, her heart pounding. "We're not going to make it!"

"Yes, we will!" Kai yelled, his voice firm despite the chaos. "Keep moving!"

With a final burst of effort, they dove out of the observatory just as the ground gave way. The structure collapsed behind them in a deafening roar; sending up a plume of sand and dust that darkened the sky.

The trio lay sprawled on the rocky ground, gasping for air. For a moment, no one spoke, the enormity of their escape sinking in.

Leo broke the silence, his voice shaky but attempting humour. "So... anyone else votes we skip the next death trap?"

Mira let out a breathless laugh, her hands trembling. "Not a chance. We've come too far."

Leo doubled over, catching his breath. "That… was too close."

Mira held the compass piece tightly, her hands trembling. "But we have it. That's what matters."

Kai nodded, though his expression remained grim. "The desert knows we're here now. It won't make the next step any easier."

Mira glanced at the compass piece, then at the endless dunes ahead. She knew he was right. The Mirage Expanse was just beginning to reveal its true challenges, but for now, they allowed themselves a moment of triumph.

The Obsidian Encounter

The desert night was unnervingly quiet. The trio's campfire cast long, flickering shadows on the surrounding dunes, but the warmth of the flames did little to ease the tension that hung in the air. Mira held the second compass piece in her hands, its polished surface gleaming in the firelight. Kai sat nearby, sharpening his knife, while Leo stared up at the stars, his usual quips noticeably absent.

Mira glanced toward the horizon. "It feels… off tonight. Too quiet."

Leo chuckled nervously. "I mean, after almost being buried alive in a collapsing observatory, I could use a little 'quiet.'"

But before anyone could respond, a low, rhythmic drumming reached their ears. It was distant at first, a faint pulse carried by the wind, but it grew louder with each passing moment.

Kai stiffened immediately, his knife frozen mid-sharpening. His eyes darted toward the darkness. "We need to move. Now."

Mira stood, alarmed by the urgency in his voice. "What's going on?"

Before Kai could answer, shadows began to materialize around the camp. Cloaked figures emerged from the darkness, their black robes blending seamlessly with the night. Each figure wore an intricately carved mask resembling a different desert creature—a serpent, a scorpion, a jackal. Their movements were eerily synchronized as they formed a circle around the trio, their footsteps creepily silent against the sand.

Leo backed up toward the fire, his eyes wide. "Uh… who invited the masquerade party?"

Kai slowly rose, his knife at the ready. "Don't move. Don't provoke them."

The leader stepped forward. He wore a mask shaped like a hawk which glinted in the firelight.

"You trespass where you are not welcome," his voice calm but dripping with threat. "Surrender what you have taken, and you may leave with your lives."

Mira clutched the compass piece tightly to her chest. "We're not here to steal anything. We're just trying to find answers about my grandmother's past."

The jackal-masked figure tilted its head as if considering her words. "The desert's secrets are not for the unworthy. You seek what you cannot comprehend."

Kai stepped between Mira and the figure, his hand hovering near the hilt of his knife. "We're not unworthy, and we're not leaving empty-handed."

The leader's gaze lingered on Kai; his voice now streaked with recognition. "You... you know of us."

Before Kai could respond, the figures began to chant, their voices weaving a haunting melody that sent chills down Mira's spine. The drumming grew louder and faster, and Mira's heart pounded in rhythm with the sound. The sand at their feet began to shift and swirl, forming a glowing, intricate pattern. Mira clutched Kai's arm. "This isn't normal, is it?"

"No," Kai admitted, his voice tight. "This is their test. And it's going to be brutal."

"Get ready to run," Kai muttered, his grip on his knife tightening.

But before they could move, the ground gave way beneath them. They plummeted into darkness, the world spinning as the sand swallowed them whole.

When Mira opened her eyes, she found herself lying on a cold, obsidian floor. The chamber around her was dimly lit, the walls glistening like polished onyx. Faint symbols glowed faintly along the walls, their shapes shifting and pulsing as if alive.

Leo groaned nearby, sitting up and rubbing his head. "What is it with us and falling into things?"

Kai was already on his feet, scanning the chamber grimly. "We're in their trial. This is how they test trespassers."

Mira stood, clutching the compass piece tightly. "Who are they, Kai? You know something about them."

Kai hesitated, his eyes darting toward the glowing symbols. "They're called the Obsidian Veil. They've existed for centuries, maybe longer. Their purpose is to guard the desert's secrets—artifacts, knowledge, ruins—anything they deem too dangerous or sacred to be disturbed."

Leo frowned. "So, they're like… the desert's secret police?"

"Something like that," Kai replied. "They don't just guard the secrets. They test anyone who tries to uncover them. And if you fail…" He didn't finish the sentence, but his expression said enough.

Mira's voice trembled. "Have you faced them before?"

Kai nodded, his jaw tightening. "Yes. Once. They nearly killed me. My father… he used to tell me stories about them. The Obsidian Veil isn't just a group—they're a force. They protect the desert's secrets with everything they have. If we're here, it means they think we've crossed a line. They're relentless, Mira. They won't stop until they're sure we're either worthy or eliminated."

The chamber suddenly rumbled, and from the shadows emerged a massive creature. Its body was feline-like, covered in fur that shimmered like molten glass. Its fiery orange eyes glowed with an unnatural light, and its claws scraped against the obsidian floor, leaving trails of sparks.

Leo staggered back, his voice cracking. "Of course, there's a giant monster. Why wouldn't there be?"

Kai drew his knife. "Stay focused. This isn't just a fight—it's part of their test. Look at the walls." "This isn't about killing it. The Obsidian Veil's trials are about endurance and intelligence. Look for the clues."

Mira turned her gaze to the glowing symbols, which pulsed brighter whenever the creature moved. "The symbols… they're reacting to it."

Kai nodded. "Exactly. They're part of the trial. We need to figure out how to use them."

The beast roared and lunged, its massive claws slicing through the air with terrifying speed. For something so enormous, its movements were unnervingly swift. The trio barely had time to react before it crashed into the stone floor, sending shards of rock flying in every direction.

Mira dove to the side as a clawed hand slammed down where she had just been. Dust filled the air as she scrambled back, her palm brushing against one of the glowing symbols on the wall.

Instantly, the floor beneath them pulsed with light, forming a faint, flickering pathway.

"It's a riddle!" Mira shouted over the chaos. "We need to activate the right sequence of symbols to create a path!"

Kai twisted midair, barely avoiding the beast's snapping jaws. "Then let's move *fast!* This thing isn't going to wait for us to figure it out!"

The creature roared again, its molten eyes narrowing as if it understood them. With a snarl, it lunged straight at Leo.

"Not happening!" he yelped, rolling out of the way just as its claws tore through the stone floor, leaving deep gashes where he had been standing a second ago. He scrambled up and slammed his palm against a glowing symbol on the pillar beside him.

A new section of the chamber lit up, revealing another piece of the glowing path leading toward a massive door on the far side of the room.

Mira dodged another attack, her heart hammering. She leaped over a crumbling bracket, barely catching her balance before reaching another symbol. She slapped it, and another piece of the path appeared.

The beast snarled, realizing what they were doing. It let out a deafening roar and charged at Kai. He barely had time to react before it swiped at him with deadly precision. The force sent him flying backward, hitting the ground hard.

"Kai!" Mira shouted, rushing toward him.

"I'm—ugh—fine," he groaned, pushing himself up. His gaze flickered to the door, then to the remaining symbols. "Keep going!"

Leo, breathing heavily, spotted another symbol and dived for it, smacking his hand against the glowing surface. "I hope this is the right one!"

The chamber trembled violently as more symbols activated, illuminating the final pieces of the path.

The beast let out a furious snarl, its molten claws scraping against the stone as it prepared for one final, devastating attack. It lunged straight at Mira, fangs bared.

She froze. There was nowhere to run.

"Hey, over here, you overgrown lava cat!" Leo shouted. He grabbed his canteen and hurled it straight at the beast's face. The metal container struck its nose with a *clang*, splashing water over its molten skin.

The creature roared in fury, shaking its head. That was all the time Mira needed. She took a deep breath and pressed the final symbol.

With a deep, rumbling groan, the massive door at the end of the chamber shuddered and creaked open. A golden light poured in, illuminating the path forward.

"This way!" Kai shouted, already sprinting toward the exit.

Mira and Leo bolted after him, their feet pounding against the glowing pathway. Behind them, the beast let out an ear-splitting roar and lunged—its claws swiping just inches from Leo's back.

Mira jumped forward, crossing the threshold just as the beast made one final, desperate attempt to reach them. With lightning reflexes, she slammed her hand against a rusted lever on the wall.

The door groaned. Then, with an earth-shaking *boom*, it slammed shut.

The beast's furious roars echoed from the other side, but the stone door held firm. The sounds slowly faded, until at last, there was silence.

The trio stood there, panting, hands on their knees as they tried to catch their breath.

Kai dusted himself off, shaking his head. "Let's agree never to mess with lava monsters again."

Mira, still staring at the sealed door, finally exhaled. A slow smile formed on her face. "That," she said, "was incredible."

They collapsed onto the sandy ground outside, gasping for breath. The stars above twinkled serenely, as if mocking the chaos they had just escaped.

Leo laughed breathlessly; his voice shaky. "If that's their version of a welcome, I'd hate to see what they do for a goodbye."

Mira held up the compass piece, its surface still warm to the touch. "We passed their test. That's what matters."

Kai's expression was sombre. "The Obsidian Veil doesn't just test your strength or wit. They test your resolve. They know we're here now, and they will do everything to challenge the journey ahead."

Mira looked out at the endless expanse of dunes, her grip on the compass piece tightening. "Let them try. We're not turning back now."

The secrets of the past were within reach, and she wasn't going to let anything stand in her way.

The Forest of Shifting Shadows

The desert had tested them with its illusions and uncompromising trial; but as they moved ahead, the landscape began to change. The golden dunes gave way to dry, cracked earth, and suddenly, a dense forest rose before them like a living wall. The towering trees were dark and twisted, their twisted branches reaching toward the sky like skeletal fingers. A thick mist clung to the air, curling around their ankles as they hesitated at the threshold.

Mira clenched the compass pieces tightly, frustration bubbling inside her. They had no way of knowing where to go next. The compass wasn't whole; without it, there was no clear direction. "We're walking blind here," she muttered.

Leo exhaled heavily. "Great. First, a death-trap desert, and now a nightmare forest. Any chance we find a cozy inn with hot meals and soft beds next?"

As they walked, Kai stared at the tree line, both amazed and uneasy. "This place... something's wrong with it. My father mentioned the Forest of Shifting Shadows. But he never said it looked like this."

"What did he say then?" Mira asked.

"That it moves," Kai replied. "Paths change, landmarks vanish. If you don't keep moving in the right direction, the forest swallows you whole."

In that moment, the ground beneath their feet shuddered, and suddenly, the narrow path they had stepped onto twisted unnaturally. The trees groaned and shifted, forming an unrecognizable new path behind them. The way they had come was gone.

"Okay. That's not normal," Leo whispered.

Before they could react, a low growl rumbled through the thick mist. Then another. And another. Pairs of glowing yellow eyes flickered in the shadows, circling them like hungry predators.

"We are *not* alone," Mira whispered, stepping closer to Kai and Leo.

From the mist, sleek creatures sneaked into view. They were unlike any animals they had seen before—large, feline-like beasts with shimmering dark fur that almost melted into the darkness. Their eyes burned with intelligence, and they moved with eerie coordination.

"We need to run. *Now*," Kai hissed.

But before they could, the creatures attacked.

The trio barely dodged as one lunged, its claws slicing through the air where Mira had been standing a second before. Another creature swiped at Leo, who yelped and scrambled out of the way. Kai slashed at one with his knife, but the blade barely nicked its shifting form.

"They're made of shadows!" Mira gasped. "How do we fight shadows?"

"We don't! We get out of here!" Kai shouted.

They sprinted down a barely visible path, dodging between trees as the creatures pursued them. The forest itself seemed to work against them, branches reaching out like grasping fingers, roots shifting beneath their feet. The beasts closed in, their growls growing louder.

Just as a massive one lunged at Mira, a whizzing sound sliced through the air. A sudden gust of wind tore through the trees, and with it came a cascade of glowing dust—like crushed moonlight—raining down upon the creatures. The beasts let out deep hisses, their shifting forms growing unstable. A hooded figure leaped down from a low-hanging tree branch, rolling smoothly onto the ground. With swift, precise movements, she scattered more of the substance into the air, and wherever it touched the creatures, their forms wavered before melting into the darkness entirely.

The forest fell into an unnatural silence.

The figure pulled back her hood, revealing a woman with sharp, striking features. Her dark hair was cropped just below her chin, streaked with silver despite her young age. Her piercing amber eyes gleamed with experience and warning.

"You shouldn't be here," she said, her voice steady and sure.

Mira, still catching her breath, eyed the woman warily. "Who are you?"

"Sylas," she answered. "And you're lucky I was watching. Otherwise, you'd be part of this forest by now."

Kai stepped forward, his grip on his knife tightening. "How do you know this place?"

Sylas let out a humourless laugh. "Because I've been trapped here for twenty years."

Leo's jaw dropped. "Wait, what? *Trapped?* Then how are you still alive?"

"I learned the rules," Sylas replied. "This forest doesn't just shift; it tests you. If you fail, you don't get a second chance. I've seen travellers wander in and never come out."

Mira frowned. "Then why haven't you left?"

Sylas hesitated, her gaze shifting toward the dense trees. "Because I didn't have a reason to. Until now."

Sylas' sharp eyes locked onto Mira. "Also, you have something precious."

Mira instinctively clutched the compass pieces closer, their faint glow barely visible through the transparent satchel strapped across her chest. "What are you talking about?"

Sylas took a slow step forward, her gaze fixed on the shimmering shards with a mix of intrigue and suspicion. "Those," she said, nodding toward the satchel. "They're no ordinary shards. I've seen symbols like them before—deep in the heart of this forest. They mark something hidden. Something powerful." She studied Mira closely. "But the Mirage Compass was destroyed. Lost in history. So tell me... *how do you have pieces of it?*"

Mira hesitated before answering. "One of them belonged to my grandmother."

Sylas raised an eyebrow, a slow smirk creeping across her face. "Your *grandmother* had a piece of the Mirage Compass?" She let out a short, amused breath. "Well then... she was either a legend—or a thief."

The certainty in Sylas' voice made Mira uneasy. Her stomach tightened and pulse quickened. "What do you mean?"

Sylas crossed her arms. "The compass wasn't just lost—it was *kept* hidden. Buried in time, erased from memory. And yet, here you are, carrying its remnants like some family heirloom." She tilted her head, watching Mira's reaction. "Makes you wonder, doesn't it? Just *how much* does your grandmother really know?"

Mira's grip tightened around the satchel. A storm of questions raced in her mind.

For the first time, Mira wasn't sure if she was holding a treasure—or the remnants of a betrayal. Before she could respond, Kai stepped forward, his expression dark with distrust.

"That's it?" he snapped. "You throw out some cryptic remark about Mira's grandmother and expect us to *go along* with whatever game you're playing?" He gestured toward the satchel. "You've been watching us, waiting for the right moment—and you suddenly decided to help? Why should we believe a single word you say?"

Sylas grinned unaffected by Kai's aggression. "I want out. And if helping you gets me out, then I'm in. But first, we have to survive," she said looking straight into his eyes.

She turned and glanced around the forest warily. "The creatures won't stay gone for long. We need to move. Now."

The trio exchanged glances before nodding. Whatever secrets Sylas held; she had just saved their lives. That was enough for now.

As they followed Sylas deeper into the shifting forest, the trees moved again, the shadows stretched unnaturally under the moonlight.

The path ahead split into three identical trails, each leading into a corridor of trees that seemed to stretch endlessly. Sylas cursed under her breath. "It's the Reflection Maze. If we take the wrong path, we'll be wandering in circles forever."

Kai frowned. "There has to be a way to tell them apart."

Sylas pulled a small vial from her pouch, its contents glowing faintly. "Watch." She spilled a drop onto the path. The liquid shimmered, then vanished entirely. "That one's fake. The forest erases anything left behind on false paths."

Mira quickly tore a scrap from her journal, dropping it onto the second path. It fluttered, but did not disappear. "This is the real one!"

They hurried forward, the other two paths collapsing into darkness behind them.

As they pressed on, the dense canopy above twisted, allowing brief glimpses of a strange, glowing mist drifting between the trees.

Mira was the first to spot movement—a cluster of translucent creatures no larger than rabbits, their elongated limbs barely touching the ground as they glided rather than walked. Their bodies shimmered like morning dew, and their large, luminescent eyes seemed to watch them with idle curiosity.

Kai grinned, lowering his voice. "These are Whisper Drifters. My grandfather used to tell me about them. They don't harm anyone, just float around collecting echoes of old voices. If you listen closely, you might hear something ancient."

Mira tilted her head, catching a faint whisper that brushed past her ears, like a long-forgotten lullaby. The creatures coiled lazily around them before fading into the mist.

Sylas, meanwhile, was inspecting the nearby trees. Small, spiralling vines were embedded within the bark, sprouting tiny clusters of violet shrubs that pulsed faintly. She plucked one and held it up. "These are Dreamroot shrubs. They only grow in enchanted places like this. Their sap enhances sight beyond illusions, but too much of it can trap you in waking dreams."

Kai ran his fingers over a nearby tree, noting how the vines pulsed with energy. "And you've used these before?"

Sylas smirked. "More times than I'd like. Some illusions here are impossible to navigate without them."

As they walked, their stomachs rumbled with hunger. Mira sighed. "I don't suppose we'll find anything edible around here?"

Sylas scanned the foliage before leading them toward a tree with twisting golden roots. Its branches bore round, deep-blue fruits with dotted silver skin. She plucked one and tossed it to Mira. "Try it."

Mira hesitated, inspecting the fruit's strange glow. "What is it?"

"Starshade," Sylas explained. "Safe to eat, but you'll feel a little light-headed afterward. It tricks your body into thinking it's eaten a full meal."

Leo bit into one with a satisfied hum. "Not bad. Tastes like honey and cinnamon."

Kai nodded in approval. "Better than starving."

With their hunger momentarily satiated, they continued deeper into the forest, unaware of the weird silence creeping in around them.

A river blocked their path, its surface spookily still. As they approached, distorted voices echoed from the water. "Come closer... rest... drink..."

Leo shuddered. "Yeah, no thanks."

Sylas crouched near the riverbank, pulling out a small, rusted coin. "The river is cursed. If you listen too long, it pulls you under. But it has one weakness—it only takes what is freely given."

She flicked the coin into the water. Instantly, the whispers turned into agonized screams as the river churned violently. A moment later, the water stilled, revealing a narrow stone path beneath the surface.

"Move fast," she ordered. "It won't last long."

They ran across the path one by one as the whispers returned louder than before.

As they reached the other side, Sylas finally spoke. "I was eight when I got trapped here. My family was the Keeper of the Desert's Secrets," Sylas said, her tone quiet but firm. "For generations, we guarded ancient knowledge—maps, artifacts, things that many sought but were never meant to find. Navigators, treasure hunters, and even kings sent people after us, hoping to capture what we knew. One night, they came for us. We fled into this forest, thinking it would protect us. We were wrong."

Kai's eyes widened as recognition dawned. He slowly stood up; his expression solemn. "Your family… The Keepers of the Desert… My father wrote about them. He spoke of their sacrifices, of how they protected history itself."

He placed a hand over his heart and gave a respectful nod. "It is an honour to stand before you, Sylas. Your kin deserved better than what they suffered."

Sylas held her gaze for a moment before offering a small, sad smile. "They did."

Mira's breath caught. "What happened to them?"

Sylas' eyes darkened. "They didn't make it. The forest kept me instead. And for twenty years, I have waited for a way out."

Sylas turned and motioned for them to follow. "Stay close. The forest doesn't like strangers."

For the first time, Sylas had a reason to believe she might finally escape. As they moved forward, the forest seemed to breathe, exhaling a chilling mist that clouded their vision. Shapes emerged—ghostly echoes of travellers who had failed before them, their hollow eyes reflecting the agony of their eternal entrapment. Shadows slithered between the trees, whispering temptations and half-truths meant to lure them into the void. The air grew thick with an unseen presence, watching, waiting. The shifting paths twisted reality itself, forcing them to rely on instinct and each other more than ever before.

Mira's grip on the compass pieces tightened as an unnatural chill crawled up her spine.

"No matter what happens, stay together," Sylas whispered.

As they walked, she explained the rules of the Forest of Shifting Shadows. "The paths change under the moonlight. If you take the wrong turn, you'll end up walking in circles—if you're lucky. If you're not, you'll end up somewhere much worse. The only way to navigate is to follow the flickering lanterns."

True enough, as they moved deeper into the trees, small orbs of bluish light appeared in the distance, floating like will-o'-the-wisps. Sylas led them toward the nearest one, but as they approached, the lantern flickered and split into separate lights, veering in different directions.

"This is one of the forest's trials," Sylas said. "Only one path is safe. The others will lead to... well, let's just say you don't want to find out."

Mira exhaled sharply. "How do we know which one to follow?"

Sylas glanced at her. "We don't. But the forest will test us. We have to figure it out together."

Kai studied the floating lanterns. "There must be a clue. Something we missed."

Leo scratched his head. "Or we could just pick one and hope for the best?"

Mira shook her head. "No. The forest is watching us. It wouldn't give us a test without an answer."

Sylas smiled. "You're smarter than you look. Let's figure this out."

Mira's fingers tightened around the compass pieces; their edges jagged where the missing sections should fit. She ran her thumb over the markings, hoping they reveal something—anything—that could guide them.

Kai crouched, examining the ground beneath the floating lanterns. "Look here," he whispered, pointing to faint depressions in the earth. "Some of these paths have been travelled before."

Sylas knelt beside him. "Clever, but it could be a trap. The forest might want us to think that's the way."

Mira studied the pieces of the compass again. Though incomplete, they still held power. She lifted them toward the lanterns, watching closely. One of the floating lights pulsed ever so slightly—almost as if responding. Her heart pounded. "I think the compass is reacting."

Leo leaned in. "You sure?"

She turned the pieces slightly, aligning them as best as she could. The faintest shimmer of light pulsed through the engravings when aimed at the brightest lantern. It wasn't much, but it was something.

Sylas exhaled. "Looks like the forest gave you just enough of a clue."

Mira took a deep breath and stepped toward the pulsing lantern. As they moved, the other lights flickered erratically before vanishing into the darkness. The air around them grew warmer, the tension in the trees easing as if they had passed an unseen judgment.

Behind them, the paths they hadn't chosen twisted and collapsed into shadows, swallowed by the forest itself.

Leo let out a nervous chuckle. "Well, I'm glad we didn't just guess."

Suddenly, the ground beneath them gave way, sending them tumbling into darkness. They landed on a cold stone platform suspended above an abyss with no end. The stars above were distorted, shifting as if caught in an unseen tide. Before them stood an ancient mechanism—an intricate puzzle of rotating rings etched with symbols.

Kai stepped forward, brushing dust from the engravings. "I've seen something like this before," he murmured, recalling the intricate maps his father once studied. "It's a celestial lock... but it's far more complex than anything I've ever seen."

The mechanism was a maze of interlocking rings, each engraved with symbols shifting under their gaze. The moment Kai's fingers grazed one of the rings, the lock spun violently, the platform beneath them shaking. Mira staggered back as golden runes flared along the edges, illuminating a new set of carvings—stars aligning, constellations blinking like living entities. The abyss rumbled, as if awakening from slumber.

Leo ran his hands through his hair. "Okay, so touching things randomly is a *bad* idea."

Sylas studied the markings, her brow furrowed. "This isn't just a puzzle—it's a test. If we don't align it perfectly, we may not get another chance."

A sharp gust of wind howled through the chasm, nearly knocking them off balance. Mira reached out instinctively, steadying herself against the ancient mechanism. As her fingers brushed a particular symbol, a beam of light shot from the engravings, striking a painting above them— revealing fragmented images of a compass, a shifting sky, and a set of rotating constellations.

Kai's breath hitched. "It's a star map! We need to align the rings to match the sky above."

Leo looked up at the distorted heavens, where stars blinked in and out of existence, shifting too fast for the naked eye. "Yeah? And how exactly do we do that before we plummet into nothingness?"

Sylas narrowed her eyes and pulled out a small vial of Dreamroot extract. "We don't *see* the sky—we *feel* it."

Without hesitation, she dabbed a drop onto her temples, then passed the vial to Mira. One by one, they followed suit. The world around them blurred, the spinning lock shifting before their eyes into a spectral display of glowing constellations. The path was clear—but the puzzle wasn't finished yet.

The rings had to be turned in a specific order, corresponding to the movement of the celestial bodies. Mira's hands trembled as she moved the first ring. It resisted at first, then clicked into place. Kai adjusted the second, sweat beading on his brow as the lock fought against him. The wind howled louder, the abyss pulling at them like unseen hands.

"Hurry!" Leo gritted his teeth as he pushed the final ring. The puzzle let out a deafening *clang*, the abyss below erupting with energy. For a moment, everything was still— then the lock began to glow, pulsing like a beating heart.

From within its depths, a compartment slid open, revealing the fourth compass piece. Mira lunged forward, snatching it just as the ground beneath them quaked. The puzzle groaned, gears grinding as ancient magic stirred to life. The abyss below thundered, and from its depths rose a staircase woven from pure starlight.

Mira clutched the piece, breathing hard. "Got it."

Kai let out a breathless laugh. "Barely."

Sylas eyed the staircase warily. "The forest isn't done with us yet. We need to move—now."

A voice, neither alive nor dead, whispered through the void. "The way forward is earned, not given. Trust is your key, or the abyss shall claim you."

The Hidden City

The celestial staircase pulsed beneath their feet. The cruel weight of the forest lifted, giving way to a strange, open landscape. The air was thick with moisture, and the scent of saltwater streaked the breeze. Before them stretched an endless lake, its surface as still as glass, reflecting the sky in an unnatural way—stars rippling across the water even though it was still daytime.

Mira stepped cautiously onto the damp shore, clutching the compass pieces. "This doesn't make sense. The map led us here, but there's nothing—"

Before she could finish, the water quivered ripples spreading outward in perfect symmetry. Then, slowly, the lake parted.

A massive structure emerged from beneath the surface. Towering pillars carved with intricate symbols rose into the air, followed by stone archways covered in glowing blue script. The water cascaded down its sides like waterfalls reversing their course. A grand gate, reinforced with thick metal bars and gears, groaned as it unlocked itself. A hidden city, submerged beneath the lake, had just revealed itself.

Leo stared. "That is *insane*. We're walking into an actual sunken city."

Kai examined the carvings on the pillars. "Not just any city. This place was hidden deliberately. My father's notes mentioned ruins like these—ancient civilizations that built defences to keep their knowledge out of unworthy hands."

Sylas whistled; arms crossed. "Looks like we're about to test if we're 'worthy' or not."

With cautious steps, they approached the entrance. As soon as they passed beneath the first archway, a deep humming sound resonated through the stone. Gears clicked into motion, and suddenly, massive figures emerged from the shadows. Towering mechanical guardians—humanoid in form, but made entirely of polished metal and glowing blue energy—blocked their path. Their eyes flickered to life as if sensing intruders.

Mira instinctively reached for her dagger. "Any ideas?"

Kai flipped through his father's notes. "They won't attack unless they deem us a threat. There should be some kind of trial—"

One of the towering guardians raised its heavy, metallic arm. A deep, grinding noise echoed through the chamber as the entire space came to life. Hidden gears groaned and screeched, shaking dust loose from the towering stone walls. Massive slabs of rock shifted, sliding in and out of place like a giant, ancient machine resetting itself.

The floor trembled beneath their feet. Suddenly, thick stone barriers shot up from the ground, cutting off pathways and creating a twisting labyrinth. Jagged spikes emerged from hidden compartments on the floor, forcing Sylas and her companions to step back. The air grew thick with tension as the metal guardians, once motionless sentries, began to move with terrifying precision.

Their bodies hummed with energy. Metal plates shifted and unfolded, revealing razor-sharp blades where their hands had been. Their glowing eyes fixed on the intruders.

Sylas' heart pounded. She scanned the shifting walls, the rising barriers, the deadly traps. This wasn't just an ancient puzzle meant to test their wits—it was a trap designed to eliminate intruders.

"This isn't just a puzzle," she said, her voice steady but urgent. "It's a defence mechanism. We should find the right path before the chamber locks us in—or worse."

A low mechanical whir filled the air as one of the giant guardians stepped forward, its blade gleaming under the dim, flickering torchlight. Time was running out.

Sylas' mind raced as the walls continued shifting, sealing off potential exits one by one. The air was thick with the grinding of stone and the relentless whirring of the guards' weapons. The floor beneath them vibrated, warning of another imminent trap.

"There!" she shouted, pointing to a narrow passage that had just opened on the far side of the chamber. But the opening was already beginning to close, the stone walls sliding together like giant jaws.

Without hesitation, she sprinted forward, weaving through the maze of rising barriers and dodging the deadly spikes jutting from the floor. The others followed close behind, their breaths ragged, their movements desperate.

One of the sentinels attacked, its bladed arm slashing through the air. Sylas barely managed to duck in time, feeling the cold metal slice a few strands of her hair. She rolled forward, landing hard on the uneven ground. The moment she looked up, her heart stopped—another sentinel stood directly in her path, its weapon raised.

She twisted to the side just as the blade came crashing down, striking the stone with a deafening clang. A shower of sparks flew into the air. Seizing the chance, she darted past, her feet pounding against the shifting floor.

The others were struggling to keep up. Kai tripped as a stone slab rose beneath his foot. Sylas turned back, grabbing his arm and yanking him to his feet just as a spike shot up where he had fallen. "Move!" she yelled.

The passage was closing fast. The gap was shrinking to barely the width of a person. One by one, they dove through, scraping past the rough stone edges. Sylas was the last.

With every ounce of strength, she hurled herself forward. The walls groaned as they met, the final gap no wider than a hand's width. Sylas hit the ground on the other side, rolling across the cold stone floor. A thunderous boom echoed behind her as the walls sealed shut, trapping the sentinels within.

For a moment, there was only silence. Then, the team gasped for air, their bodies trembling from adrenaline.

Sylas lay on her back, staring at the ceiling. "That," she panted, "was too close."

Mira let out a breathless laugh. "Next time, let's try a door instead."

Steadying their breaths, they pressed onward, their footsteps echoing through the silent passage ahead. The air was thick with the weight of something unseen, as if the ruins themselves were watching. The further they went, the more the stone corridors began to change.

Then, as they stepped beyond the last archway, the ruins unfolded into something grander.

The group moved forward into the heart of the city. Grand spikes stretched toward the sky, some still submerged, with bridges connecting them in twisting patterns. Strange globes of glowing energy floated above their heads, casting a dim, ethereal light. The city was alive in ways they couldn't understand.

At the centre stood a grand hall, sealed by an enormous metallic door covered in shifting engravings. Mira's compass pieces vibrated.

"The next piece is behind this door," she murmured, her voice barely above a whisper.

Leo ran his hands over the carvings, tracing the unfamiliar symbols. "There's no handle. No keyhole. So how do we—"

While he spoke, the engravings began to move, twisting and rearranging before their eyes.

Something was awakening.

Mira stepped back as the engravings twisted and pulsed. The ancient door was alive.

Leo jerked his hand away. "Uh… I don't like that."

Kai drew his daggers, scanning the area. "This isn't just a door."

Sylas tilted her head, studying the shifting patterns. "Or a lock. And we need the right key."

Mira glanced at the compass pieces in her hand. They were vibrating with increasing intensity, glowing faintly at the edges. Slowly, she raised them toward the door. The engravings responded immediately, the shifting metal forming a circular scoop in the centre.

"I think…" Mira hesitated, then pressed the compass pieces into the slot.

The moment they touched the surface; a deep hum filled the air. The engravings stopped shifting. Then, with a loud *click*, the symbols rearranged themselves into a single, glowing inscription.

Leo squinted. "Can anyone read that?"

Sylas stepped closer, brushing her fingers over the luminous text. "It's ancient. But I recognize parts of it." She took a deep breath and read aloud:

"To enter, the lost must be found. To awaken, the seeker must sacrifice."

Mira's stomach twisted. "Sacrifice?"

Before anyone could react, a gust of wind burst from the door seams, sending dust and loose debris flying. The compass pieces in Mira's hand pulsed violently.

Then, the door demanded its price.

The glow spread outward in pulsing waves, and the grand hall shuddered as if the stone itself had taken a breath. The intricate carvings lining the walls twisted as if awakening from an ancient dream.

Then, from the stone itself, a deep groan echoed through the chamber.

A mass of black mist unfurled, coiling and expanding, its form flickering between shapes—one moment an eagle with tattered wings outstretched, its ember-like eyes burning into Mira's, the next a twisting serpent, its smoky body spiralling through the air, then a horned beast with jagged, shifting limbs, clawed hands stretching toward her. It never settled, never remained whole, as though it existed in many forms at once, flaming like a broken image on an ancient reel.

Its hollow gaze locked onto Mira, a predator recognizing its prey.

The chamber trembled as the creature moved without sound, its presence bending the air around it. The weight of its stare pressed into her chest; the flickering light of the chamber swallowed by its shifting void-like form.

And then it lunged.

Mira instinctively stepped back, but the door pulsed again, and an invisible force locked her in place.

"The seeker must sacrifice," Sylas muttered. Then, her eyes widened. "Mira—it's not asking for blood. It's asking for *a piece of you.*"

Mira barely had time to process those words.

A sharp, freezing pain shot through her chest as the darkness wrapped around her wrist. Memories flashed through her mind—her grandmother's voice, the smell of old parchment, the moment she found her first artifact. The shadow-like-mist was *pulling* something from her.

Mira clenched her teeth, fighting the force. "Not happening."

Summoning all her strength, she slammed her palm against the engravings. When her skin made contact, a searing golden light erupted from the compass pieces still embedded in the door. The shadow shrieked, recoiling from the blinding glow. The entire chamber trembled.

A wave of energy blasted outward, knocking them all off their feet.

Then—silence.

Leo was the first to sit up, rubbing his head. "Okay. That was dramatic."

Sylas pushed herself up, brushing dust off her scraped palms.

The shadows were gone. The grand hall was still.

Kai peered into the dark opening where the grand door had once stood, its shattered remnants still crackling with fading light. "Well," he said, brushing dust from his sleeves, "that was fun. What's next?"

Mira didn't answer right away.

She was still on the ground, heart pounding, her hair tossed in disarray from the blast of wind that had thrown them all back. Her gaze was locked on the swirling air ahead, where the door had vanished.

Then she felt it—a faint pressure against her chest.

Slowly, she reached for the satchel strapped across her torso, her fingers trembling. As she unfastened the flap and peered inside, her breath caught.

The compass pieces.

All three of them were nestled there, untouched, their glow pulsing gently like a steady heartbeat. They had returned on their own.

Her stomach twisted in awe and unease.

"Mira?" Leo's voice broke through, cautious. "You okay?"

She looked up, eyes still wide, but a steely calm settling into her voice. "They're here. The pieces… they came back."

Kai raised an eyebrow. "Seriously?"

She nodded slowly. "Whatever just happened… it's not over."

Then, with her jaw set and fingers tightening around the satchel strap, she stood.

"Let's find out what's waiting."

With no other choice, they stepped forward into the unknown. The air was thick with the scent of damp stone and something old—older than the ruins themselves. Flickering torchlight cast restless shadows along the towering walls, revealing elaborate carvings etched into the stone. Symbols. Stories. Warnings.

Leo let out a shaky breath. "Okay. That was officially the worst welcome I've ever had."

Kai smirked. "You say that every time."

Mira, however, wasn't listening. Her eyes were fixed on something ahead—a pedestal in the centre of the chamber, partially hidden beneath layers of dust and tangled roots. Resting atop it, gleaming faintly under the dim light, was a fragment of the compass they had been searching for.

She stepped forward, drawn to it. The others followed cautiously, still on edge from the last trap.

"Be careful," Sylas warned.

Mira hesitated for only a second before reaching out. The metal was cool beneath her fingertips. She lifted the piece, and a low rumble vibrated through the floor.

But this time, something else was stirring.

A slow, deliberate clap echoed through the air. A tall figure clad in dark, feathered armour emerged from the shadows of a crumbling archway A mask shaped like a raven's beak concealed his face, his piercing eyes glowing beneath the shadow of his hood.

Kai tensed. "The Raven."

Mira's breath caught in her throat. There was something unsettlingly familiar about the way he stood, the way he spoke.

"You've come far," The Raven said, making his way down the bridge with slow, deliberate steps. "But you have no idea what you're truly chasing. That compass holds more than you realize." He tilted his head, his voice laced with intrigue. "It seems your grandmother... hasn't told you everything."

Mira's fingers tightened around the compass. "What do you know about my grandmother?"

The Raven took another step forward. "Everything."

"I must say, you're more resourceful than I expected. But you're playing a game you don't understand."

Mira clenched her jaw. "How dare you."

The Raven spoke in a teasingly accusing tone. "Oh, Mira. I thought you'd be happier to see me. After all, your grandmother and I go way back."

Mira stiffened. Her grip on the compass tightened. "Liar."

"Oh, but she never told you, did she?" The Raven stepped closer. "About the real reason she spent years chasing these artifacts? About the truth hidden in the Obsidian Veil?" He smirked. "This compass isn't just a key. It's something your grandmother never wanted to be found."

Before Mira could react, a deafening *boom* shook the ruins. The floor cracked beneath them, and a deep, wide crater split the chamber into two. From the darkness below, a rush of cold air blasted upward, carrying the scent of something ancient… something alive.

Then came the sound—a rough, bone-rattling roar.

Mira barely had time to grab Leo's wrist before the ground crumbled beneath their feet. They fell into the crater.

The Descent into the Abyss

The wind howled in Mira's ears as they tumbled through the void. Stone debris rained around them, vanishing into the endless black below.

"Hang on!" Kai shouted; his voice barely audible over the roar of the wind. He twisted midair, tossing a hook toward a sharp crest. The hook latched onto the rock, the rope pulling taut. He swung hard, catching Leo's arm just as the boy waved helplessly in the freefall.

Sylas reached out, fingers closing around Mira's wrist. The force nearly pulled her shoulder out of its socket, but she gritted her teeth and held on.

They slammed against a sloping rock wall, sliding fast. Sparks flew as Kai's hook scraped the stone, struggling to hold. The crater stretched endlessly below, but then—

A massive, serpentine shape burst from the darkness.

Its scales shimmered like molten silver, reflecting the dim glow of their torchlights. Rows of razor-sharp teeth gleamed as the creature lunged, its glowing blue eyes locking onto them.

"A sky serpent?!" Leo shouted in disbelief.

"Not the time for questions!" Sylas yelled back.

The serpent struck, its jaws snapping inches from Mira's foot. She flipped onto her stomach and rushed toward an elevation of glowing crystals.

"Jump!" Kai shouted.

No time to think. They pushed off the rock wall just as the serpent's tail whipped past, slicing through the air where they had just been.

Mira crashed onto the ridge, rolling to absorb the impact. Leo landed beside her, groaning. Kai and Sylas tumbled down moments later. The glowing crystals pulsed beneath them, casting an unnerving blue light over the cavern.

The sky serpent circled above, its massive wings keeping it aloft. It wasn't leaving. It was waiting. Hunting.

Then, from the shadows of the cavern, a hundred smaller glowing eyes flickered to life.

Mira's breath caught in her throat.

Leo exhaled a shaky breath. "Oh… that's not good."

From the cracks in the rock walls, dozens of winged creatures began crawling out—small, bat-like beasts with clawed hands. Their eyes glowed with the same light as the serpent above.

Kai tightened his grip on his daggers. "Run?"

Sylas nodded. "Run."

The Race Through the Cavern

They bolted, leaping over pointed rocks and skidding down narrow ledges as the creatures swarmed behind them. The serpent let out another ear-splitting roar, its body twisting through the cavern as it dove toward them.

Leo fumbled in his satchel, yanking out a handful of small, metallic spheres. "Cover your ears!"

He hurled them over his shoulder. The spheres hit the ground—then exploded in a blinding flash of light and deafening noise. The creatures shrieked, scattering in all directions.

"Nice work!" Mira shouted.

"Don't celebrate yet!" Kai called back, pointing ahead.

The path ended at a sheer cliff. Below, a rushing underground river roared, vanishing into the unknown.

"Jump or die!" Sylas shouted.

No time to hesitate. They leaped into the void, plunging toward the river below as the sky serpent's jaws snapped shut just behind them.

The icy water swallowed them whole.

The Compass Completed

Darkness. Silence. The current dragged them down, twisting, spinning—until suddenly, they burst into an air pocket, gasping for breath.

They had survived.

For now.

The river carried them through a narrow tunnel, its waters glowing faintly from the crystals embedded in the rock walls. Mira struggled to keep her head above water as the current tossed them forward. The last thing she remembered before being pulled under was The Raven's voice echoing in her mind: *This compass isn't just a key. It's something your grandmother never wanted to be found.*

Then, as suddenly as they had fallen, they were expelled from the underground river. The water spat them out into a shallow basin surrounded by moss-covered ruins. Coughing and shivering, they pulled themselves onto the rocky shore.

Leo groaned, rolling onto his back. "I am so done with ancient death traps."

Mira turned to the others, dripping and breathless. "We need to find out what The Raven knows."

Leo shivered. "Preferably before another ancient monster tries to eat us."

Sylas squeezed the water from her cloak, scanning their surroundings. "Where are we?"

Kai, still breathless from their escape, sat up and looked around. "If my father's notes were right… this is the last trial."

Sylas exhaled. "Let's move before something else wakes up."

As they climbed toward the surface, Mira clutched the compass pieces tightly. The Raven had answers—answers she needed. But one thing was clear. They had come too far to turn back now.

The path leading to the ruins twisted through a breathtaking landscape that seemed untouched by time. Towering crystal formations jutted from the ground, glowing softly in hues of blue and violet, casting a dreamlike glow across their surroundings. The air shimmered with bubbles of golden light, shifting and spiralling as if alive, guiding their way forward.

Every step they took seemed to stir the whispers of an ancient world. Strange flora lined their path—flowers with petals of translucent silver that hummed gently when brushed, vines that pulsed faintly, tracing their movements. The deeper they ventured, the more the atmosphere changed, as if they had stepped between two realities.

As they ventured deeper into the ruins, Mira's gaze was drawn to a tree unlike any she had ever seen. Its branches were lined with long, delicate feathers instead of leaves, each one shifting subtly as though caught in an unseen breeze. The feathers beamed with a rainbow-like sheen, and as she stepped closer, a gentle hum echoed from its trunk.

Kai noticed her staring and followed her gaze. "That's no ordinary tree," he murmured. "Feathered trees like this were said to mark sacred sites in lost civilizations. If this is here, it means we're close."

Leo took a step back. "So, you're saying this tree is directing us toward something important?"

Sylas nodded. "An altar, most likely. Ancient places of power were always marked in ways only the keen could recognize. We need to keep moving—this tree is a sign we're on the right path." The air shimmered ahead of them, as though disturbed by an invisible force. At the same time, faint tremors pulsed beneath their feet, rhythmic and deliberate.

Kai placed a hand on the ground, closing his eyes. "This isn't natural. The vibrations… they're in a pattern. Almost like a message."

Leo huffed. "First haunted forests, now the ground is talking? What's next, a riddle from the wind?"

Sylas shot him a glance before kneeling beside Kai. "No, he's right. The pulses are deliberate. They're forming a sequence."

Mira studied the terrain, her mind racing. "A sequence... like coordinates?" She glanced down at the compass pieces in her hand, noticing how they faintly pulsed in sync with the vibrations. "The compass is reacting to it. It's trying to tell us something."

Kai's brow furrowed. "Then if we match the pattern with the map, we should be able to pinpoint the exact location of the altar."

Leo crossed his arms. "Great. So, we just have to follow the invisible drumbeat of the earth? Easy."

Sylas smirked. "For once, you're not wrong."

Using the subtle tremors as their guide, they adjusted their course, weaving through the towering ruins with growing anticipation. The energy in the air thickened, making it clear they were getting closer.

After hours of following the tremors and keeping an eye on the shifting symbols in the ruins, exhaustion began to take its toll. The path ahead grew steeper, and the ruins became more difficult to navigate. The rhythmic pulses in the ground hadn't changed, but they felt no closer to their goal.

Mira sighed, rubbing her temples. "We can't keep moving like this without rest. One of us should stay awake while the others take turns sleeping. We don't know what else could be lurking in these ruins. If the altar is nearby, we should be sharp when we reach it."

Kai hesitated before nodding. "She's right. If we push ourselves too hard, we might miss something important."

Sylas scanned the area before pointing toward an overhanging stone structure covered in glowing moss. "There. That should give us some shelter for the night." The ruins loomed in the distance, waiting for them. They made a small fire, its light flickering against the pointed rock walls. The heat felt unnatural, crackling in a way that sounded almost musical.

Leo stretched his legs, wincing. "I can't believe we're almost there. Feels like we've been running forever."

Sylas tossed a small bundle of dried fruit toward him. "We rest now, but at first light, we move. Something tells me the final stretch won't be easy."

Kai sat cross-legged, absently running his fingers over the carvings on the stone floor. "This place is different from the others. It doesn't just feel old—it feels awake."

Mira held the compass pieces close, watching the glow reflect in the firelight. "Then we should be ready for anything."

They drifted into an uneasy sleep, the soft hum of the ruins around them like a distant lullaby. But the moment the first light of dawn touched the horizon, a deep tremor ran through the ground beneath them.

The ruins called them forward.

The mist thickened as they approached, curling around their legs like unseen hands. Every step toward the ruins carried a weight, an unspoken warning. Strange symbols carved into the surrounding stones flickered in and out of visibility, as if responding to their presence.

They finally reached the place where the ruins around them stretched high into the misty air, their carvings worn by time but still pulsing with faint energy. At the heart of the ruins stood an altar—ancient and unyielding. At its centre was a circular dent, the exact size of the compass pieces Mira carried.

Kai noticed it too. "That's where it goes."

Mira hesitated. The weight of everything that had led them here settled on her chest. "What if The Raven was right?" she whispered. "What if this is something we were never meant to find?"

Sylas placed a hand on her shoulder. "Then we decide for ourselves. Not him. Not your grandmother. Us."

Leo smirked, trying to lighten the moment. "Besides, if we went through all that just to chicken out now, I might cry."

Taking a deep breath, Mira stepped forward. The compass pieces felt warm in her hands as she placed them into the dent one by one. The moment the final piece clicked into place; a deep hum vibrated through the air.

The symbols on the altar glowed, spreading outward like veins of light. The carvings on the walls responded illuminating ancient writings that had been lost to time. The ruins trembled—not in destruction, but in awakening.

A column of light shot into the sky, piercing through the mist. Above them, the stars shifted, rearranging themselves into constellations they had never seen before. The ground beneath them pulsed like a heartbeat, and then, with a final surge of energy, the altar released a golden, glowing object from its core.

It was the Mirage Compass. Whole. Complete.

Mira reached for it, and the moment her fingers brushed against its surface, the visions struck.

She gasped as images flooded her mind. A great city, floating above the sands, lost to time. A war fought in secret, between those who sought to protect its knowledge and those who wanted to claim it for themselves. A woman—her grandmother—standing at the heart of it all, hiding the compass away.

And then… darkness. A warning. *What is revealed cannot be undone.*

Mira stumbled back, her breath ragged. The visions faded, but the unease remained.

Kai caught her before she could fall. "Mira? What did you see?"

Mira looked at them, her voice barely a whisper. "This compass… it doesn't lead to treasure. It leads to something much bigger. And if we follow it… there's no turning back."

Sylas frowned. "Then the real question is… do we?"

The compass pulsed in Mira's hands, as if waiting for her answer.

She tightened her grip, her heart pounding. This was it. The final choice.

Mira exhaled slowly, then met their eyes with quiet resolve.

"We go."

And as the compass's glow surrounded them, the ruins began to shift once more, revealing the path to their next journey—the truth hidden beyond the Mirage Expanse.

The Final Truth

The compass pulsed in Mira's hands, the golden glow casting flickering light against the ruins as they stood at the threshold of the unknown. The ancient structure before them was unlike anything they had encountered—a colossal archway carved into the rock, half-buried in the desert sands. Strange symbols ran along its surface, shifting and rearranging themselves as if alive, forming a language long lost to time.

Sylas ran a hand over the inscriptions. "This is it," she murmured. "The entrance to the Veiled Vault."

Kai studied the markings closely. "The vault where Zorath vanished. My father's notes always said the place was a myth. No one who entered ever came back."

Leo huffed. "Fantastic. Another place people don't come back from. We have a habit of walking straight into those, don't we?"

Mira tightened her grip on the Mirage Compass. "No turning back now. If this place holds the truth about my grandmother, I need to know."

As she lifted the compass toward the archway, its glow intensified, casting beams of light that connected with the shifting symbols. The ancient carvings groaned in response, unlocking mechanisms buried beneath the sand. The ground trembled as the archway split open, revealing a spiralling staircase descending into darkness.

Kai exhaled sharply. "Well, that's an invitation if I've ever seen one."

The air grew colder as they descended, the only sound their cautious footsteps echoing through the tunnel. The deeper they went, the more the walls changed—smooth sandstone gave way to dark, polished stone etched with intricate patterns. Glowing blue veins pulsed within the rock, like the very walls were alive, watching their every step.

They finally reached a massive circular chamber. At its centre, a pedestal stood bathed in a soft, ghostly glow. Upon it rested an obsidian tablet covered in the same shifting script as the archway above. Surrounding the pedestal, massive statues of cloaked figures loomed over them, their faceless forms exuding a creepy presence.

Mira approached the pedestal with bated breath, her fingers tracing the edges of the obsidian tablet. The moment she touched it, a pulse of energy rippled through the chamber. The statues' eyes flared to life, glowing with deep amber light.

Then, a voice—neither entirely human nor entirely spirit—echoed through the vault.

"You seek the truth of the Mirage Compass. Know this: knowledge is a double-edged sword. What is revealed cannot be undone."

Mira clenched her fists. "I don't care about warnings. I need to know what my grandmother was hiding."

The air around them shimmered, and suddenly, the chamber transformed. The walls became translucent, revealing visions from a time long past. They stood in the midst of an ancient city—a city floating above the sands, its towers gleaming under twin moons. People in flowing robes walked through the streets, their hands adorned with rings bearing the same symbol as the Mirage Compass.

And at the centre stood Zorath.

He was younger than Mira had imagined—his dark eyes sharp, his posture regal. But it was the woman beside him who made Mira's breath hitch.

"That's... Amma," she whispered.

Her grandmother stood at Zorath's side—chief of the Obsidian Veil—her expression unreadable as she held the Mirage Compass in her hands. The people around them bowed in reverence, their gazes filled with awe and fear.

Then the vision *shifted*.

Mira gasped as she was pulled into another time, another place.

She stood on the edge of a vast desert, the land cracked and lifeless beneath a merciless sun. Zorath raised the compass, and with a single turn of its needle, water surged from the barren earth, weaving into rivers that slithered through the wasteland. Parched soil darkened, sprouting lush greenery in an instant. Trees stretched toward the sky, their leaves unfurling like they had been waiting an eternity to breathe again. The desert had *come alive*.

But then, the vision twisted. The compass struck, and the rivers raged, no longer a gift but a curse. The calm streams swelled into monstrous waves and cities drowned beneath the churning waters. The very people who had once rejoiced now screamed for mercy as the floods swept them away.

The scene blurred again.

Now, Mira stood in a dense jungle, thick with ancient trees and the hum of unseen creatures. A weary traveller knelt before the compass, his body wracked with fever, his breath shallow. Zorath traced a path with the needle, and instantly, the forest *answered*. Vines parted, revealing a hidden grove where golden-hued leaves glowed softly in the dim light. The traveller reached out, crushing a single leaf between his fingers, and within moments, colour returned to his face.

But before Mira could process the wonder of it, the vision darkened once more.

The compass spun wildly, and the same golden leaves, once healing, blackened and shrivelled. The air grew thick with decay, and a deathly silence replaced the jungle's song. Figures emerged from the shadows, their faces gaunt, their eyes hollow. A disease spread like wildfire, consuming the land, turning the once-thriving forest into a graveyard of twisted, lifeless branches.

The compass could *give*, and it could *take away*.

Mira's chest tightened as the visions merged into a swirling storm—the compass shaping mountains, splitting oceans, guiding the lost, cursing the greedy. A tool of creation. A weapon of ruin.

And then, just as suddenly as it began, the storm of images shattered.

She was back in the burning city.

The once-glorious skyline was ablaze. Shadows spread like a plague, consuming buildings and twisting the skies into darkness. The same robed figures who once bowed in reverence now fought amongst themselves—half trying to protect the compass, the other half desperate to claim it.

Mira stood stunned, her pulse pounding. *This* was why the compass had been hidden. Not just because of its power— but because power like this could never be truly controlled.

She barely had time to breathe before the vision pulled her deeper.

Mira's grandmother was at the heart of the battle, her hands raised as she chanted in an ancient tongue. Zorath reached for her, shouting something Mira couldn't hear. But before he could stop her, she twisted the central dial on the compass and threw it into the air.

A blinding light erupted from its core, engulfing everything in its path.

The vision shattered, and Mira staggered back, gasping. The chamber was silent once more.

Kai's face was pale. "Your grandmother hid the compass to keep it out of their hands."

Leo ran a hand through his hair. "And Zorath... he was part of all of this. He wasn't just some myth. He was real."

Sylas folded her arms, her expression unreadable. "And now we know why The Raven was after you. He wants to finish what your grandmother started."

Mira looked down at the Mirage Compass, its glow now subdued, as if exhausted by the weight of the truth it had revealed. "She wasn't trying to protect a treasure. She was trying to bury a secret for the sake of mankind."

Kai exhaled. "Then the real question is... what happens if we uncover it completely?"

Silence filled the chamber. For the first time, Mira wasn't sure she wanted to know.

But she realized one thing was certain. There was no escaping it now.

The Decision

The air inside the Veiled Vault still crackled with the lingering energy of the Mirage Compass. Mira's hands trembled as she clutched the glowing artifact, its pulsing light illuminating the dust-laden chamber. Her heart pounded as the weight of her discovery settled upon her— her grandmother had betrayed the Obsidian Order to keep the compass safe.

"It doesn't only reveal ancient places," Mira whispered. "It reveals the truth."

Kai wiped the sweat from his forehead, staring at the inscriptions along the chamber's walls. "Which means it could change everything. Expose every hidden city, every buried secret…"

"Or destroy the world as we know it," Sylas finished grimly.

Before Mira could respond, the air suddenly shifted, heavy with the presence of something unseen. Then came the sound—footsteps. Slow, deliberate, and echoing with authority.

"The Obsidian Veil," Kai muttered, reaching for his dagger.

Shadows melted into form as cloaked figures stepped into the chamber, their leader standing at the forefront. The Raven. His dark, feathered armour gleamed in the compass's glow, his mask concealing everything but piercing, knowing eyes.

"You've done well, Mira," The Raven said smoothly, his voice laced with quiet menace. "You've proven yourself far more capable than we anticipated. And now, it's time for you to hand over the compass."

Mira tightened her grip around the ancient artifact. She stared at him, unflinching. "You could have killed me way back and taken it. Why didn't you?"

The Raven chuckled, tilting his head slightly. "Ah, now *that* is the right question." He took a slow step forward, his dark cloak shifting with the movement. "You see, child, the Mirage Compass is… selective. It can't be found by those who seek to *use* it. Only by someone who doesn't know its purpose—or doesn't *want* to use it."

Mira's breath caught in her throat. The realization hit her like a wave. "That's why my grandmother never told me about it."

A slow, knowing smile spread across The Raven's lips. "Exactly. She *knew* you would search for it if she left you in the dark. It was the only way to make sure it ended up in your hands." He let out a quiet, almost amused sigh. "She was clever. I'll give her that."

Mira felt her pulse quicken. Her grandmother had set this in motion. Not by guiding her—but by *trusting* her.

Leo stepped forward, his fists clenched. "So what? You think that means she wanted you to have it? Not happening."

The Raven chuckled again, dark amusement flickering in his eyes. "Oh, no! She didn't want *me* to have it." His gaze snapped back to Mira, sharp as a blade. "But she was never quite certain about *you*."

Mira's stomach twisted, but she forced herself to stand firm. "I don't care what you think," she said. "I'm not giving it to you."

The Raven exhaled, almost disappointed. "Ah, Mira. If only it were that simple."

Mira took a step back, gripping the artifact tighter. "You want to control it."

"We want to use it for what it was meant to do," The Raven corrected. "Imagine a world without secrets. A world where no power hides in the shadows. No empire hoards its treasures. No lies go unchecked."

Sylas scoffed. "That sounds a lot like control to me."

The Raven turned his gaze to her. "You, of all people, should understand, Keeper. Your ancestors hid truths that could have reshaped history. And for what? So the powerful could remain powerful? So the world could stay blind?"

Kai stepped forward. "Some truths are hidden for a reason."

The chamber trembled as if the compass itself was reacting to the tension. Mira looked down at the artifact in her hands, its swirling energy shifting like an unsettled storm. The power to reveal everything—every lost civilization, every untold history—was within her grasp. But at what cost?

Mira's grandmother had kept this secret for a reason. If the wrong people got their hands on it, the balance of the world could be shattered.

But if she destroyed it now… would she be any different than the Obsidian Veil, deciding what should and shouldn't be known?

Her mind raced.

She needed to outsmart The Raven.

Mira took a deep breath and met The Raven's gaze. "Alright. You want the compass?"

She lifted it, letting its golden light fill the room. The members of the Obsidian Veil leaned forward, anticipation gleaming in their eyes.

Then, with a swift, decisive motion, she twisted the central dial on the compass and threw it into the air.

For a heartbeat, time seemed to slow. The compass hovered, its glow intensifying as it spun. Then, a blinding pulse of light exploded outward, shaking the very foundations of the chamber.

The Obsidian Veil recoiled, shielding their eyes. The walls trembled, and ancient mechanisms groaned to life. Sand and stone cascaded from the ceiling as Mira dived for Kai and Sylas, dragging them toward the nearest exit.

The light consumed the chamber, the very fabric of reality seeming to ripple. Then, with a final, deafening crack—the compass split.

The Raven staggered forward, his mask slipping slightly. "No!" His voice was raw with fury.

Mira turned back for just a moment, meeting his enraged gaze. "Some secrets aren't meant for anyone."

The ground beneath the Obsidian Veil fractured, and the vault collapsed in a torrent of dust and rubble. Mira, Leo, Kai, and Sylas sprinted through the crumbling passage, barely making it to safety as the ancient chamber sealed itself behind them.

They collapsed outside, gasping for breath.

Kai exhaled. "You destroyed it?"

Sylas studied her carefully. "Or did you hide it?"

Mira looked down at her hands. The Mirage Compass was gone—shattered, its power dispersed. Only a single, dull fragment remained, resting in her palm. But something deep inside her told her it wasn't truly lost.

She took a slow breath, the words slipping from her lips like a forgotten melody, ones she had heard long ago in the soft glow of lamplight, wrapped in the warmth of Amma's voice.

"A flame may flicker, but its warmth never fades. A river may break, but its waters always find their path. And a treasure never truly disappears—only waits to be found again."

She looked up, her gaze steady. "It's safe," she said simply.

Kai exchanged a glance with Sylas, uncertainty flickering in his eyes. "Safe *where?*"

Mira closed her fingers around the fragment, feeling its faint hum. She didn't need to explain. Some things weren't meant to be spoken—only understood.

Amma had always known. The stories weren't just bedtime tales. They were *preparations*. And now, Mira finally understood why.

A New Legacy

Mira's footsteps echoed softly as she stepped into her grandmother's study. The scent of parchment and aged ink filled the air, a smell she had known since childhood. The dust of their adventure still clung to her clothes, but something inside her had changed. She was no longer just a girl searching for answers—she was a seeker, just like Amma had been.

Carefully, she slid the compass piece into a hidden compartment, its glow fading as it settled into place. She stood, running her fingers along the wooden desk, tracing the faint marks left behind from years of study. The room felt different now, not just a relic of the past, but a place where stories were still being written.

Leo's voice broke her thoughts, pulling her back. He was standing in the doorway with Kai and Sylas. "You okay?"

Mira turned to face him, a small smile tugging at her lips. "Yeah. I think I finally understand why she did it."

Leo raised an eyebrow. "Amma?"

She nodded, her gaze softening. As she set the map on the desk, she murmured, "She was a seeker. Not just for artifacts, but for answers. For stories. For something more." She walked over to the window, gazing at the horizon, where the sun dipped low, casting a warm glow over the town. "I've always wanted to know what drove her, but I never understood it until now."

"Mira?"

The warm, familiar voice made her turn.

Amma stood in the doorway, leaning slightly on her cane, her sharp eyes taking in Mira's dishevelled state. There was no surprise on her face—only knowing understanding, as if she had been expecting this moment.

Mira swallowed the lump in her throat. "I found it, Amma. The compass. I know the truth."

A long silence stretched between them before Amma stepped forward, resting a gentle hand on Mira's shoulder. "And what will you do with that truth, child?"

Mira exhaled slowly, the enormity of the journey settling over her. "I hid it. It's too powerful. Too dangerous. Some secrets should stay buried."

Amma nodded, her expression unreadable. Then, a small, proud smile touched her lips. "Good."

Leo, Kai, and Sylas appeared behind her, watching the exchange with quiet respect.

Mira met her grandmother's gaze, realization dawning. Amma had never chased mysteries for power or recognition—but for the journey itself, rising as a true guardian.

Mira turned to the study table and her fingers traced the edges of the ancient map she—the map of **Kalanya**. The name felt heavier now, its meaning tangled with everything she had just experienced. She took a slow breath before speaking.

"Amma," she said carefully, "how is Kalanya connected to all of this? The hidden places, the lost cities, the Mirage Compass... What does all of it mean?"

Amma ran a gentle hand over the map, her expression unreadable.

"Kalanya is not just a place, child," she murmured. "It is a whisper carried through time, a secret held by those who dared to seek the unseen. 'Kala'—time. 'Anya'—endless. It exists between what was and what will be, waiting for those who listen."

Mira felt a chill dance up her spine. "So it *is* real?"

Amma smiled, the kind of smile that held riddles rather than answers. "Some say Kalanya is a city lost to time. Others believe it is not a place at all, but a path—a journey taken only by those who are truly ready to see."

Mira tightened her grip on the map.

"So if I follow this..." she trailed off, watching her grandmother closely.

Amma chuckled softly, brushing Mira's hair back as she had when she was younger. "Then be careful what you seek, my dear. For in Kalanya, the past does not stay buried... and neither do its secrets."

Mira swallowed, a thrill of anticipation racing through her. She had thought her journey had ended, but now, she wasn't so sure.

She looked at the map again, the ink seeming to shift under the lantern's glow.

Maybe... it was just the beginning.

Mira looked at her friends—Leo, who had stood by her since the beginning; Kai, whose knowledge had guided them through the most impossible challenges; and Sylas, who had shown them what it meant to survive against all odds. They had all changed. They had all found something out there in the ruins and shifting sands.

She turned back to Amma, determination in her eyes. "I think I want to keep going. There's still so much out there."

Amma's smile warmed. "Then go, child. Find your path." She turned toward the kitchen, her voice light with affection. "Wait right here. I have something for you—my special creations. You must be starving after all that adventure."

Leo clapped his hands together. "Well, if we're doing this again, I'm making a list of things we should avoid."

Sylas smirked. "Trusting mysterious strangers in masks."

Mira laughed, her heart swelling with warmth. "Noted."

She turned back to the study, her eyes landing on an old map pinned to the wall; one that her grandmother had marked with countless red X and cryptic symbols. Unlike before, when she had stared at it in longing, now she saw it for what it was—a challenge, an invitation.

The compass was just the beginning. She could feel the pull of the unknown once more. With her heart set on the future, she turned back to Leo, Kai, and Sylas. "There's a whole world out there. And I'm going to find it."

The group stood in silence for a moment.

Then, just as Mira stepped toward the door, ready to embrace whatever came next, the room seemed to shimmer. The ancient map gleamed with life, and the candlelight flickered, casting moving shadows over the map, as if it, too, was waiting for her next step.

And in the distance, far beyond the familiar lands she knew, something new and unexplored began to glow, waiting for the next seeker to answer its call.

The world was still full of mysteries. And she intended to find them.

As she stepped forward, a new legacy had begun.

About the Author

Isha J. (Dr. Isha Jaswal) is an acclaimed academic and emerging storyteller whose passion for discovery and detail brings her stories vividly to life. With a Ph.D. in Economics and a rich career spanning research, writing, and global teaching, Dr. Jaswal has spent years exploring the complexities of human nature, societal shifts, and hidden truths—a journey that naturally flowed into the realm of fiction.

The Mirage Compass, her debut children's novel, is a heartfelt tribute to curiosity, courage, and the thrill of the unknown. Woven with mystery, magical realism, and emotional depth, it follows a young girl's discovery of a lost legacy and the secrets hidden just beneath the surface of the everyday.

Inspired by the wonder of childhood imagination, Isha J. crafts stories that empower young minds to seek, question, and believe. She brings to fiction the same thoughtful precision and wonder that have defined her scholarly work—only now, through secret maps, forgotten cities, and glowing compasses.